THE ROCKER THE BOY AND ME

NIKKI PINK

DEDICATION

Dedicated to YOU, my fabulous readers

Lucy

I pouted my lips and twisted a lock of my blond hair around my finger. It was in vain — I knew the professor didn't swing my way and I didn't think he had the power to help anyway — but it was all I had.

"Please, if I can do that course I can graduate early. I can't afford another semester. I can't."

Professor Gains took off his glasses and rubbed his eyes. "I know that, Lucy. But you know I don't make the rules. In order to graduate you need at least six more credits directly related to Business Communications. And for the summer session, the classes are either full or you've already taken them. These other classes," he paused as he looked at the list of classes I'd suggested, "Anthropology 201, Ballet, the Shakespearean Sonnet — don't meet the requirements for your major. I'm sorry, but you're not going to be able to graduate early."

I sighed. It wasn't fair. It wasn't. I'd registered for

the final two courses I needed to avoid another semester of tuition, but the professor who was supposed to be teaching them had been in a car accident, and now they weren't going to be offered this summer.

"It's not fair," I said with a groan.

"I know, my dear, I know. Life's not fair."

I slumped in the chair with my head drooped and shoulders hanging limply forward. "I guess I'll be seeing you again next semester then."

He nodded. "Yes, but—" He frowned. "I'm afraid I have some more bad news."

My head whipped up sharply. More bad news? What the fuck? "What...?"

"You'll only be taking six credit hours related to your major next semester, so you won't be eligible for the academic scholarship you've been receiving thus far. That scholarship is only available to those taking a *full* course load."

"What the hell?"

"I'm sorry. You know I don't make the rules. I agree it's ridiculous."

"That's really, *really* not fucking fair."

He rubbed at his temples, his brown eyes giving me a look of sympathy. "I know. I know."

What else could he say? Not much. I was glad he didn't try and rationalize the college's stupid policy.

"So I have to pay tuition? Like, all of it?"

He nodded sympathetically. "Yep. I can recommend you for a couple of smaller scholarships. I can probably swing those. But you will be responsible for the bulk of your tuition."

"You've seen my GPA right? I only came to this overpriced college because I knew I could keep my scholarships." *Calm, Lucy, calm. It's not his fault.*

He nodded sympathetically.

I smashed a fist into the palm of my other hand. I was frantic. This was such bullshit.

"Know any strip clubs hiring?"

His eyebrows shot to the top of his forehead. "What!?"

"Well my family sure as shit ain't got the money. A girl's gotta do what a girl's gotta do..."

"Lucy!" He had a panicked look on his face.

I giggled, amused by his shocked reaction. "Hey,

it might be fun."

I was only teasing him, I wasn't going to become an exotic dancer just to earn a few month's tuition. Was I?

"Thanks anyway, Prof."

"Please, don't do anything you'll regret. You're eligible for all kinds of loans. Some of the federal loans are pretty low interest too."

I nodded. "I know. I know. It's just I really, *really* wanted to graduate without any debt. I'm so close. So close. It's just a pride thing."

He closed his eyes and nodded. "Well, please. Consider all your options. Don't do anything you'll regret."

I nodded and rose to my feet, revealing my long legs which had been hidden behind the desk. Not that they did me any good with this professor.

"Thanks anyway. I guess I'll be seeing you again next semester."

He rose to his feet and offered me a hand. He shook my hand delicately He was a very gentle man and I felt comfortable with him. Even when he was pissing me off.

"Have a good summer, Lucy."

"You too, Professor," I said and gave him a grin.

I span on my heels and sashayed to the door, swinging my ass the way a stripper struts across the stage. When I got to the door I looked over my shoulder and saw a panicked look on the professor's face. I blew him a kiss and walked out.

* * *

I pulled Nicole's chair away from the desk and placed it in the middle of the room. "Here, come sit down."

She gave me a strange look like she didn't trust me. She was my roommate and best friend but she always guessed when I was up to something, though this time I could tell she wasn't quite sure what mischief was about to ensue.

"Why?"

"Just do it, okay? Why do you always want an explanation for everything?"

"Because I know you!" she said in an accusatory tone. But she did as she was told and sat on the chair anyway. Of course she did. She's my best friend, and the only person I trust in the world.

I pressed *play* on my phone and through the magic of wireless technology music began to start blaring out of the speakers on my desk. A sexy *Beyonce* number.

Nicole raised her eyebrows at me and I grinned as I raised my arms up and began to dance to the beat, all swinging hips and shaking bosom. Not that I had much to shake up there, but hey, I worked with what I had.

"What are you doing?" she asked.

I didn't reply but gave her my most smoldering look. Her cheeks began to flush and I hid a giggle. She was still so uptight, despite having lived with me for three years. And becoming a biker club president's old lady.

For her, anything vaguely sexual should be kept hidden from prying eyes. Despite this, I knew she'd done it in a warehouse, rooftop and even the back of a motorcycle. I guess she didn't care as long as no one was watching.

I placed two arms behind her neck and pushed my

breasts near her mouth. That did it.

Nicole shot to her feet, pushing me away. "What the hell are you doing?"

I grinned at her. "Pretty hot, huh?"

"So, what, are you going to be a stripper now? Decided the world of business isn't for you?"

I laughed and collapsed onto the bed behind me. "No. But I just found out I need to do another semester. No early graduation for me. And no scholarship either. Gotta' get me some tuition money."

"Shit. Really?" Her look of annoyance had turned to one of concern. She knew how hard I'd worked toward early graduation, and to maintain my scholarships.

I gave a nod. "Yeah. So, I figure I need to get a loan or earn some money. And you know how I feel about loans."

"I'd get a loan," said Nicole, "rather than... that."

I giggled. "Don't you think it'd be fun, though? Dancing's fun, right? Why not get paid for it? Why don't we do it together, huh?"

She let out a laugh. "You think Jase would go for

that?"

I frowned. "Yeah... maybe not."

Her boyfriend, Jase, was the president of the Sons of Mayhem motorcycle club and was fiercely protective of her. While he'd no doubt enjoy her dancing for *him*, if it was for someone else... well, let's just say you wouldn't want to be that someone else. Unless you were into pain. And not the sexy kind. More the *am I ever going to walk again?* kind.

"Anyway, don't make any rash decisions yet, okay? Let's just enjoy the next couple of weeks and then see what turns up."

"Yeah, I guess. You packed?"

Nicole nodded. "You?"

"Nearly," I lied. I hadn't started. But it wouldn't take long. We were going away for a couple of weeks with a British rock band called *The Full Force*. Nicole's boyfriend's friend's friends... or something like that. The MC were going to be providing security, and so Jase was taking his old lady, aka Nicole, aka my roommate, along too.

And do you think I was going to let Nicole go off

on tour with a rock band without me? She was tied down to Jase already, she wouldn't even get to have any real fun with the rockers. There was no way in hell I was going to miss the chance to party with some sexy-accented British rock stars. No way.

As I began to throw some things into a bag I decided to forget about college for now. This next couple of weeks was about fun, not stressing over money.

I wonder what these rockstars look like. I hope they're hot. Toned torsos, sexy tats, crooning voices and hard di—

"Lucy? You ok? You zoned out again."

I flashed her a grin. "Sorry. Nearly done."

As I finished up packing my thoughts were only on the next few days. I had no idea that I was about to embark on an adventure that would flip my entire world upside down, shake it up like a tossed salad and spit me out in delighted confusion 5,000 miles later.

Lucy

"Oi, Juicy!" said Lonnie, the token British member of the Sons of Mayhem MC. *Juicy* was what some of them called me. Cute nickname, no?

"Yeah?"

"Wanna meet a rockstar?"

I raised an eyebrow. "What, you mean those guys?" I said gesturing toward the stage where they were warming up.

He nodded. "Yeah. The singer. He wants to, err…" he paused as if snatching words out of the air, "go on a date with an American girl."

I snorted. "Go on a date with? Really?"

He shifted uncomfortably. "Yeah. And I think he likes blondes. Just if you're interested..."

In his right hand he was clutching a piece of paper. Interesting. *Very* interesting. He didn't see I'd seen it.

I stepped into him, letting his eyes fall into mine

as I gave a little mischievous smile. He was so easy to distract. He didn't know what the hell I was doing until it was too late and I'd snatched the piece of paper out of his hand.

"Oi! Give me that!"

I giggled and turned my back on him, quickly unfolding it. He reached around me but I twisted away while I scanned the contents of the piece of paper.

"What the hell is this?" I yelled at him.

His eyes went wide. "I didn't write it, Chad Chad Price did." He had given up trying to get the paper away from me. I'd already seen its brief contents now.

"Who the fuck is Chad Chad Price? He sounds like a douche."

Lonnie let out a little chuckle. "Yeah. He is. 'Chad Chad Price so nice they named me twice' is what he calls himself. He's the tour manager for the band."

"And so why'd he give you this?" I said shaking the paper at him.

"I'm security. And it's security's job to... y'know..."

"Find groupies?" I asked. I looked down at the

paper again:

Groupies!!!

* *Red-headed girl-next-door, 21 max, PURPLE t-shirt*

* *Skinny Blonde. Airhead. Big tits.*

* *Bi-sexual nineteen year old Asian identical twins.*

* *MILF, 40+ BIG GIANT TITS.*

* *Sexy, wild, American girl. Blond.*

"So what, the last one is me, huh?" I asked him, my eyes fierce.

"Well—"

I stepped into him. "You think I'm wild, huh?"

He gulped. Why's it so easy to make men flustered? I just don't get it. All it takes is a pout of the lips, a slight smoldering in the eyes and standing a touch too close and they turn into putty in your hands. Even tough-guy bikers.

"And sexy?" I licked my lips slowly. "Do you think I'm sexy, Lonnie?" My voice was a throaty whisper.

"You're," his voice sounded strangled, "alright."

Alright? Dumbass. I'm not *alright*, I'm hot as a

habanero in the Texas summer sun. Whatever. I wanted to meet these rockers anyway.

"Okay. I'm in. I'll hang out with the rockstar guy for a while."

"You will? Great. He's a nice guy, I promise."

"Oh, he is?" I said, sounding disappointed.

Lonnie let out a chuckle. "Not *that* nice, don't worry, he won't bore you."

I giggled. "Glad to hear it. And tell him I'm not a groupie."

His gaze shifted away. "Right. Yeah. Will do."

I knew he wouldn't. Whatever. It might be fun to shock this rockstar who thinks he's getting some borderline-obsessive super-fan who'll hang on his every word instead of me: A shit-kicking genius who might just give him way more than he can handle.

"Later, Lonnie." As I walked away I swished my hips and then glanced over my shoulder. He was staring at my ass. Of course.

* * *

"So, what, Lonnie just asked you to hook up with *him*," said Nicole, gesturing with her head toward the stage where the band was playing.

I nodded and gave her a dig in the side. "Pretty awesome huh? He's sexy isn't he?"

I saw Nicole giving the shirtless singer an appraising look. She couldn't criticize that six foot and change toned and ripped rock star, could she?

"A bit pretty, isn't he?"

She could. I ran my eyes over him again. He was good looking, sure, and he had a great, almost ethereal voice, but he definitely was not pretty. "What are you talking about?"

"Well you know. Compared to..." Her voice faded away into the music as her words trailed off.

I frowned. Why'd she have to go and bring that up? There had been a guy, another one, in the MC. I hadn't spent long with him, just a couple of weeks, but shit had happened and he wasn't around anymore. Dead.

I hadn't known him long enough to be too badly fucked up by his passing, but it had messed me up just a little more than I already was. I didn't need it brought up again.

But Nicole was right, that guy, Brodie, had been more of a man's man - all engine grease, heavy beard, and workhorse muscles. But hey, I was allowed to go for different types of guys, wasn't I? You can't lock yourself down to just one flavor. It's a big wide world and there's a veritable smorgasbord of types of hotness out there. And I want to try every last dish. Y'know, without being *too much* of a slut.

"Sorry, I didn't mean to... " said Nicole.

I nodded and gave her a squeeze. "I know." She'd only brought me down for a moment. I wasn't going to let a wound from the past make me depressed today. If I wanted to be brought down all I had to do was think about my upcoming tuition bill for next semester. But nope, we were here to P - A - R - T - Y.

"Come on," I said as I grabbed my roommate's hand, "let's mosh."

"I don't think—" she started, but I was already dragging her through the small but crowded venue to the front where the more dedicated fans were bouncing up and down.

~You fill my needs / When you're on your knees~

the singer blared.

Would that be me, I wondered? Would I be filling his needs tonight? We'd have to wait and see whether this good looking singer deserved to get lucky with me.

Johnny

Not bad. Not bad at all. For the first show of our little mini-tour in the US it had gone pretty damn well. Although it was a small venue our manager Chad Chad Price had assured us he had a plan and that we actually *wanted* small, sold out venues to make a buzz or something. I dunno. Business isn't really my thing.

"Hey. You're Johnny, right?" said a sultry voice in my ear. It had the exotic tinge of an American accent, just like the ones you hear on the telly. Brilliant.

I looked down at the girl who'd sidled up beside me. Now *that's* what you call a proper American girl, I thought. A real cheerleadery type with a good hint of naughtiness for good measure. Long blond hair, tits bursting out of a too tight t-shirt, a plaid mini-skirt, legs a couple of miles long, half covered by black leather fuck-me boots with dangerously high heels. *Nice.*

Matty boy - or Lonnie as they seemed to call him here - had done well. Real well. "Sure am, sweetheart.

And what's your name?"

She gave me a sexy little smile. This is the life. This is the *fucking life*. Hot groupies on tap? Shit, I thought, I've made it. I've finally made it. There were plenty of women who'd throw themselves at the singer of a little-known band back home, but the problem was that they weren't necessarily the women you *wanted* throwing themselves at you. And the ones *you* liked weren't interested in the singer of an unsuccessful/up-and-coming rock band. So to get a little filly of this quality begging for it was really something. I could definitely get used to this.

She gave me a coquettish smile but her eyes sparked with something that promised pure dirty filth underneath. Her lips parted a moment before she spoke and they looked so deliciously plump I just wanted to start sucking on them immediately. I probably could, I thought.

Shit, she's a groupie who's here for me. I can do what I want! "Lucy," she paused and she turned the level of filth in her eyes up to 11, "or sometimes they call me *Juicy*."

I gulped. Fuck it. You only live once and I'm a goddamned rockstar now. I decided to go for it and leaned in for the unasked for kiss since she was obviously there for me.

Her eyes went wide as my lips approached hers. She opened her lips again as if to meet mine. I closed my eyes and—nothing. Just air. But then—

"Fuck!" I yelled. She had turned her head away at the last minute leaving me kissing the air while at the same time using one of her hands to grab my crotch. And not grabbing in the sense of giving you a tasty little frottaging through the jeans, but more like an I'm-going-to-rip-your-balls-off-y'bastard grab.

"You can't just go kissing girls you've barely met," she said.

What the hell kind of groupie was this? "But I thought—"

She gave another little gentle squeeze and I stopped thinking. She pressed her mouth right up against my ear, her hot breath in that sensitive spot sending shivers right through me. "You can stop thinking now. I'm going to tell you how it's going to be."

Huh. Just who had Lonnie hooked me up with? Here's how it usually works:

1) I do a gig, rock out on the stage.

2) Weird girls throw themselves at me.

3) I choose the least-offensive one, and wham-bam-thank-you-maa'm I have a brilliant night.

So this Lucy bird was throwing me right off. But do you know what? I kind of liked it. It intrigued me. I had become used to women just trying to please me, doing whatever I wanted just because I could strum a few tunes on a guitar and carry a tune with my passable voice. But this girl. Huh. She didn't seem impressed at all. It looked like I'd have to earn it. Just what the hell kind of groupie was she?

I decided I'd play along with her game for awhile, let her boss me around a bit. But not too long. I was going to take control eventually when I had enough of her games. Then she'd get a taste of a real man.

Lucy

I almost couldn't believe the nerve of him, just going for a kiss before we'd even spoken properly. The asshole must have been used to girls throwing themselves at him, but that's not me. Sure I have my share of fun, but don't make the mistake of thinking I'm *easy*. I'm not easy, I'm just willing to take what I want, do what I want, do *who* I want without giving a fuck about other people's or society's opinions. But that doesn't mean I'm not particular.

Now, this rockstar, this Johnny? Shit, when I saw him up on that stage, the whole crowd moving to his rhythm, carried by his voice, his music - I wanted him.

But when I met him after and he just went for a kiss like that? Nuh uh. Now he was going to have to get back in my good graces. Treat me right and I'll give you the time of your life. Treat me like a piece of meat and I'll rip your balls off and use 'em as fishing bait. Not that I know how to fish - but hey, I can learn.

I relaxed my grip around the crotch of his jeans, but as I did so I let my fingers give a little squeeze just above, feeling the outline of his pleasingly sized cock.

His eyes went wide again. He didn't know what to think. Good. That's how I like to keep men when I first meet them - confused and on edge, but *interested.*

"Okay, Johnny, why don't you take me to the bar at your hotel. Buy a girl a drink first, huh?"

I saw a twinkle in his eye at the word *first.* Good. He may have pissed me off a little but that didn't mean I no longer wanted to have fun with him.

"Alright."

Just one word. On the stage the words had been flowing out of him like honey from a gallon jug. But I'd wrong-footed him and now he was having to rapidly reassess everything he knew about young women.

"What are you smiling at?" he asked.

I let out a giggle and covered my mouth. "Nothing. Let's go."

He nodded and flicked a strand of hair out of his eyes. His right arm went behind me and his hand gave me a push in my lower back. I love it when a man guides me like that. I hadn't wrongfooted him so much he'd been emasculated - I'd just knocked him off kilter a little.

He guided me out of the club toward the tour bus. In the dark of the parking lot his hand drifted down over my mini-skirt and up my thigh again to the soft flesh of my round buttocks. He gave a sharp squeeze and I let out a giggle and let his hand linger for a second before slapping it away.

Good.

He had some proper fire in him. I smiled secretly in the dark. This was going to be fun.

Jamie

I let my blond hair fall across my brow before raising a hand to pretend to brush it away. In reality what I was really doing was wiping away a tear. But boys don't cry, do they?

Let's have an open relationship, she'd said.

Let's fuck other people and tell each other about it, she'd said.

And now what had happened to us? She'd dumped me. Now I had no one, and nowhere to go.

At first the whole 'open relationship' idea had been just fine with me. I was way too young to be settled down and there were plenty of people I wanted to get with. And that was the problem. There were about twice as many people as there should have been. And she didn't appreciate that.

Just half an hour ago we had been lying in bed together. Naked. Each lying on our back, me with one arm resting under her neck, my hand idly playing with her breasts, tracing little circles around her nipples and giving the occasional squeeze. She had a hand around my turgid cock. We'd just made urgent, frantic love after coming back from a night out — separately — and now we were telling each other about our adventures.

She'd told me about the young guy she'd sucked off at a Hollywood party filled with other wannabe actors, models and singers. About the boy's gorgeous six pack abs, and long and thick and smooth hard cock.

"That's so hot," I said.

"What about you, did you get lucky?" she asked as she gently pulled at my cock, stretching it out before wrapping her hand back around it.

"Yep," I said and the thoughts flashed back through my mind. Although we'd only just finished fucking I could feel myself getting hard again as the hot memories flooded through my mind.

"Who was it? Was she hot? Was she a pretty little starlet? Did you tell her you could get her a part if she just offered up her tight little virgin pussy for—"

"What? No!" I said.

She let out a throaty laugh. "Ohhh. Was it an

older woman? A divorcee? Or maybe one still married to an overworked and overweight producer who can't get it up anymore?"

I let out a laugh. "No. Just shut up a minute and I'll tell you."

She ran a hand up from my knee to my thigh before holding my growing cock in her hand again.

"So I was at this placed called the Red Room, do you know it?"

I could sense her frowning in the darkness. "No..."

"Yeah, we've never been there together. Anyway, that's where I met Kris."

She was using her fingertips to massage me now as I became harder at the memory. "Yeah. Anyway, after, like, half a drink we snuck out the fire-escape for a moment."

"Just half a drink? You dirty, horny, boy!"

I grinned in the dark. "Yeah well we were both horny. Of course *I* was thinking of *you*."

She laughed. "Of course you were."

"I was! Anyway, as soon as we were on the fire

escape we started making out, jeans pressed tight against each other. Frantic grabbing and squeezing and touching. But it wasn't enough."

I could hear a schlicking sound and realized she was fingering herself as she listened to my story. I gave a squeeze to her nipple and she let out a gasp. She was really getting off on this whole open relationship thing.

"So," I continued, "I dropped to my knees and got that belt open and fly unbuttoned as fast as I could. As the jeans dropped to the floor I couldn't believe my eyes..."

She let out a moan. "Did she have a pretty pussy? Was it slick and wet? Did you make her cum with her tongue?"

I let out a laugh.

"No! Kris wasn't a girl, it was a guy! Anyway, when I had his pants and boxers down his massive cock sprang up. I just couldn't help myself. I cupped his balls with one hand and I just wrapped my lips around his head and took as much of it as I could into my mouth."

It felt so good to share this with her. "Babe, you would have *loved* it, he was so hot and hard in my mouth, and he kept doing this, like, hot groaning and moaning. I didn't really know what I was doing but when he grabbed my hair I knew he liked it."

My cock was rock solid again and now it was my hand that was wrapped around my member as I squeezed it and jerked my hand up and down. I hadn't noticed she'd gone quiet.

"I think I must be a natural - I just, like, instinctively knew what he'd like - because he didn't last long! I swear it was less than two minutes before he grabbed my hair tight and filled my mouth up with his hot man juice. Shit, now I guess I know why *you* get off on blowjobs so much, babe. It was awesome! I tried to swallow all of it down but some of it dribbled down my chin; I had to wipe it off with my finger afterward. He wouldn't let go of my hair and release me until I'd milked every last drop from him. God, it was so amazing, having that boy pulsing into my mouth while he let out these long, slow moans..."

I'd gotten carried away and hadn't realized she hadn't spoken in a while. "...Babe?"

"Shut up. Don't talk to me."

I gave her breast a squeeze. "What? What's the matter?"

"I said shut the fuck up."

My blood ran cold. What was the matter? This is what she'd wanted, wasn't it? An open relationship where we'd tell each other about our conquests. Right?

"Babe, baby, did I do something wrong?"

"You know what? Why don't you just get the hell out. You're making me sick. I can't deal with this shit right now."

I felt my cock disappearing as my arousal was extinguished like a match in the ocean. I struggled to understand just what the hell was going on. "Get out? Go where?"

"I don't care. Maybe your faggot friend's house perhaps? Just fuck off. I can't believe you. I really can't."

I slipped off the bed, gathering my scattered clothes in a daze. I never should have agreed to this open relationship crap in the first place.

I pulled on my boxers and jeans. "When... when can I come back?"

She let out a sound of disgust. Who *was* this girl I was living with? I thought I knew her, but then... "I don't want you to come back. I thought you were a *man* for fuck's sake. Not some fuckin' fruit. Just get the hell out. I'll put your shit in a box. It'll be on the curb in the morning."

"Okay." My voice was a broken whisper, barely audible as I struggled to come to grips with my whole world crashing down.

That's how I found myself sitting on the curb waiting for my friend Donna to come pick me up. She'd let me crash on her couch a day or two, I guessed. But what then?

Why had I ever moved in with her? We'd only hooked up a few times; you could barely even call it dating. Of course we called ourselves a couple, but it had been all too fast really. It had seemed so logical to move in to her place. My lease was ending, hers had just begun, and we were in love. At least that's what I'd thought four weeks ago. Then she suggested the open relationship, and then when I took advantage? This shit!

I smashed a fist down on the curb and regretted it immediately. Stupid concrete. My hand was filled with a dull ache when Donna's car pulled up a moment later.

"Honey, I'm so sorry. Get in."

I nodded and climbed into the passenger seat. She wrapped an arm over my shoulder and then I couldn't take it any more. I started to sob.

Fuck *boys don't cry*.

Lucy

I was curious. I'd never met a famous person before. Not that this guy was *super*-famous or anything, but he was getting there. Might blow up soon and become a mega-star.

"So what do you do, when you're not on tour?" I asked. We were sitting across from each other at a booth in the hotel bar.

He drummed his fingers on the tabletop. "We practice, we jam, we work on new tunes..."

"So, you just play music. Like, all day?"

"Actually no, not really. It's more like crazy bursts every now and then. Someone will come up with something — a line, a riff, a beat, a vision and then we'll go all out for an hour, or two, or a day, or a coupla days, 'til we get it figured out. Sometimes we'll have a new song in half an hour. Sometimes it'll take a week. Sometimes we'll go weeks with nothing new. Some weeks we'll come up with a dozen tracks."

I nodded. It wasn't very organized, I thought. It's funny, most people don't realize it but I'm a pretty organized person, and I like to follow my systems. People see me as this wild girl doing crazy shit all the time but they don't understand me. They don't understand me at all.

Sure, I have fun. More fun than most anyone I know. But you know what? I get straight A's in all my classes. Never hand a paper in late. Was all set to graduate early. But I still party harder and do more crazy shit than anyone I know.

Sometimes people think Nicole is the organized sensible one, and she keeps me on track. Nah. if it wasn't for me hustling her she wouldn't get half as much shit done. And why am I so organized? Why do I hassle Nicole so much to get shit done? because I want to P - A - R - T - Y.

When they make a college yearbook I know they're going to put some shit like 'Most Unexpected 4.0', under my picture when it'd be more apt to put "Most Misunderstood Person on Campus." But fuck 'em. It makes people underestimate me. And that's a powerful thing.

"What do you do for fun. Just making music?"

He grinned. "Actually, it's not very rock 'n' roll, but..."

I raised my eyebrows at him. This was it, we were getting to the meat of him.

"I meditate. I do yoga. And I try to eat healthy. I even tried being vegan for a bit. That didn't last though."

"No shit? You're right, that's not very rock or roll, is it?" I tapped my chin thoughtfully. "Do you do *anything* rock 'n' rollish?"

He gave me a look. The kind of look you remember. The kind of look that has a wicked glint and promises to do things — if you dare allow it. His head moved across the table close to mine. His voice was low, as if he was telling me a secret. "I make girls like you very, very, happy."

I started to giggle but I caught myself. He had my interest piqued. "And just how do you do that?" I said to him, my voice low and sultry now.

His head tilted slightly to the side. "With these,"

he held up two hands, "with these," he said and pursed his two hot lips and blew me a kiss across the table, "and, most importantly," he said as he took my left hand in his and moved it under the table. I leaned over as he pulled me toward him by his hand. "With this," I found myself involuntarily biting my lip as he pressed my hand against his crotch. I could feel him thick and growing hard through his jeans.

My eyes caught his and then I was locked in, unable to turn away. That glint. That dreamy trap. It was impossible to break his gaze so instead I lost myself in the dark blue of his eyes and squeezed him through his jeans.

How had he done that, I thought, as I realized I was suddenly very, very turned on. I had to fight the urge to crawl under the table and release his cock right that very second.

No, Lucy, be good. You're in control here. I released my grip on his bulging crotch and pulled my hand away.

I grasped my drink and raised it to my lips, taking a sip and trying to look confident. He wouldn't get to me.

"Pretty cocky, huh?" I said.

"That's what you like, isn't it?"

I looked down into my drink but couldn't help but smile. He was so right.

* * *

I was biting my bottom lip and twisting a lock of hair around my finger and neither action had been deliberately contrived. This was pure animal flirtation, not calculated seduction.

I knew all the tricks alright. I knew that fiddling with the hair is a sign of interest, as is 'inadvertent' touching and gentle teasing. I've used all these tricks with careful deliberation in the past, taking advantage of every last skill I had to get ahead in life.

Sometimes you have to use your brain, your smarts, but sometimes you find yourself in a situation where you're not respected for your intelligence; the man you're talking to couldn't care less whether you were as smart as Einstein or dumb as a stop sign. When you're dealing with an asshole like that you have to be smart in another way — you have to use your femine wiles to get your point across.

So I've learned everything. I can argue Nietzsche or discuss Six Sigma implementation in the corporate space if I need to, or if I'm talking to a shallow sexist pig I can simply flutter my eyelashes, feign interest and grasp their forearm. Whatever works, right?

But now, I wasn't in control. My flirtations weren't carefully considered moves to get my way. Nuh-uh. This was just pure woman responding to pure man.

He raised his eyebrows at me. His voice was like warm treacle. "What are you thinking?"

Lame question. Didn't matter. It was him speaking. "What do you think I'm thinking?"

His lips spread in a knowing smile. "Oh I know exactly what you're thinking."

"You do, huh?"

He nodded, his eyes glinting mischievously as he maintained eye contact. I felt myself flushing.

"You're thinking," he leaned in close, "you're thinking, 'how long is he going to make me sit here before he takes me up to his room?'"

"Was not," I said, my voice barely a whisper. That hadn't been exactly what was on my mind, but...

"You are *now*," he stated accurately.

Some girls would brush that off in a flurry of denial. But I ain't some girls. He'd caught me. Time for the offensive. "Yep. So how long?"

He cocked his head to the side for a moment before standing up and stepping around to my side of the table. He was all lean strength and beautiful face towering over me. What's he going to do, I wondered.

I should slow him down, I thought, stay in control. Make him buy me another drink. I don't want to seem too easy. *Should*. Shoulda, coulda, woulda.

My mouth opened to speak but before a sound could escape he placed a finger over my lips. I stopped.

Then, casual as you like, he reached down into my side of the booth. I wasn't sure what he was doing at first and began to squirm away. He stopped that by placing two strong hands tight around my waist and lifting me bodily into the air.

"Oh!" I let out involuntarily as I sailed through the air before being slung over his shoulder. Damn, he had some strength in him.

He stood up straight and I found myself hanging in the air looking at the ground. My legs were in front of him and he had a strong arm wrapped around my upper thighs. My hands were dangling with my torso over his back. I grabbed his belt for balance as he strutted across the room, carrying me as his prize.

The world was confusing upside down but I could see people were staring. Not *some* people. *Everyone* in the bar. I didn't care though. Fuck 'em. It's not every day you get slung over the shoulder of a hot rock star who literally isn't afraid to take exactly what he wants.

He carried us across the lobby to the row of elevators.

"You can put me down now if you like," I said.

"Nah. It's alright." Instead of putting me down he used his free hand to run across the smooth skin of my legs, up my calf, over the back of my knee which tickled and sent my leg twitching, and then higher, onto my thigh. An involuntary shiver passed through me as the elevator dinged and the doors began to open right as his hand cupped the curve of my ass.

A man in a suit with a gold nametag marched out just as Johnny's hand reached the curve of my buttock. I realized my mini-skirt wasn't covering much of anything deposited up on his shoulder, and I guess the man in the suit realized the same. His eyebrows shot up. "Sir! Please!"

Johnny let out a laugh as he walked past the man into the elevator. "No, find your own. This one's mine."

"That's *not* what I meant—" said the voice outside the elevator as the doors closed.

Johnny gave my ass a squeeze and I let out a little yelp. "I guess that was the manager," said Johnny as he wrapped his hands around my waist again and lifted me off his shoulder. "Didn't seem too happy."

Instead of placing me onto the ground he pushed me against the mirrored wall of the elevator, my ass resting on the railing that ringed each of the three walls. Two hands under my t-shirt, pressed against my hot bare skin, held me in precarious place.

"Thanks for showing everyone my ass," I said, trying to regain my composure.

He grinned. "A beautiful little ass like yours is a

piece of art. Everyone should get to enjoy it."

I was about to retort but before I could he was standing in real close, between my legs, and one of his hands had left my stomach to grab a fistful of my hair.

I gasped as he pulled my head back and stood over me, my face directly below his.

"No escaping this time."

He was right. There was no escaping this time. Not that I wanted to. His mouth lowered to mine and our two pairs of hot damp lips pressed together.

For a split second I thought it was going to be a slow, tender kiss, but we were both too worked up for that. I grabbed onto the back of his head for both support and to pull him in closer to me. Our lips touched and broke and touched and broke in a flurry of urgent, excited noisy kisses.

I let out a moan as the hand on my stomach dropped under my skirt to my thigh, his thumb just an inch or two away from my wet pussy as he grabbed me tightly to hold me in place.

I moaned loudly as our tongues met and slid excitedly against each other before parting again. He nipped at my bottom lip eliciting another moan.

Then the elevator dinged. Stupid elevator. We'd reached the top floor.

"Bollocks," he said as he guided me down.

I stood on shaky legs and wondered how presentable I looked. Not very, I imagined.

He grabbed my hand, interlocking our fingers as he led me out of the elevator.

"Which room?" I asked.

"Royal suite," he said, before looking down and catching my eye, "Princess," he finished with a cheeky grin.

"I'm no princess," I said with a giggle.

"No?" he asked, sounding disappointed. "I heard princesses are *wild* in bed.

Johnny

Now that was more like it. I was back in control and now she was going to do my bidding.

We walked down the hallway to the double-door that led into the Royal Suite. I flashed the card at the reader, the little light lit up green, and I grabbed her hand again to lead her in. Her hand was warm and she was breathing a little fast, a little heavy. She was desperate for me. As I was for her.

"Come on," I said.

She pattered in behind me as we entered the large suite. It was sumptuous. Thick carpets, antique furniture, space to swing half-a-dozen cats. It was gorgeous.

But my eyes weren't on all that crap. After a quick glance at the massive room I turned around and looked at her. My girl for the night. I shook my head slowly.

"What?" she asked.

"Nothing," I stumbled. Goddam she looked good. I could have eaten her up right then and there. How can birds do that? Make you just lose your breath and your mind and turn you into a gibbering idiot. It didn't make sense. *I* was the rockstar here, it should have been her losing her mind over me.

She reached out a hand to mine and pulled me deeper into the room. Across the other side was a large open door through which was the large king sized bed that looked big enough to fit half a dozen girls like Lucy. Although that sounded fun in theory I doubt any man could survive *that*. I'd be lucky to keep up with this little minx by myself. She led me across the room quickly, almost running. I barely had time to take it all in.

"Come on," she said, "I'm so hot for you right now." Her tone was breathy and sultry dripping with promise.

"Yeah," I said, "I know you are," I finished lamely. I couldn't think straight.

We reached the entrance to the bedroom and she pulled me inside, spinning around and pushing our bodies into each other. I thought about picking her up and tossing her straight onto the bed, but decided to give it a minute.

She looked up at me, eyes wide, and blue as could be. "You still want me?"

I nodded. "I'm going to have you."

"You are, huh?" she asked, her voice low and sultry with just a hint of teasing. "Whether I like it or not?"

I nodded. "Take off your top."

She raised her eyebrows slightly. "Just like that?"

"Yep."

She cocked her head at me for a minute, then grabbed the bottom of the shirt that clung tightly against her torso and pulled it up over her head.

I swallowed deeply. That body. Just my type. I wanted to kiss and lick and hold and grab and pinch and caress and squeeze every last millimetre of it. I reached out two hands and ran them over her soft, soft, skin, making her giggle at my touch. It almost seemed like my hands were trembling.

"Now what?"

"This."

I reached behind her and quickly unfastened the straps of her bright red bra. I let it drop to the floor. She didn't raise her arms to cover her breasts, didn't turn around or shy away, didn't complain. Instead she ran her hands up slowly over her stomach and cupped the bottom of her breasts, not a hint of shyness or embarrassment.

"You like?"

They weren't big, but they were round with two perky, hard nipples jutting out, like two little berries waiting to be plucked, perhaps by my lips.

I leaned in and she offered her lips, but I turned down and kissed the soft, side of her neck instead. She let out a low moan. I kissed her again, on the collar bone, and then again just below. Her body was shaking gently as I continued my journey of a thousand kisses down until I reached the gentle curve of the top of her breast. She let out a low moan as I kissed the upper half of first one breast, then the other, ten, twenty, I don't know how many times.

She lifted slowly up on her toes, urging the

delicious berry of a nipple to my parted lips. I hovered over it a moment, then let out a long slow breath. The young girl let out a frustrated yelp. See, I thought, I was definitely back in control now.

"Suck it, goddamit," she said.

Before I could respond she grabbed the back of my head and yanked my hair, trying to force my lips onto her waiting, quivering breast. You gotta love a girl who knows what she wants in the bedroom and isn't afraid to go for it. But that doesn't mean you have to give it to her. Not if you want to tease the little cocktease yourself and get her so hot and wet she thinks she'll melt or die of horniness.

She was strong, but not as strong as me. I kept my lips just above her hard little nipple and blew a taunting breath of air over it as she let out a frustrated yelp.

This girl wasn't one to not get her own way though and her next move nearly brought me to my knees. She wrapped both hands around my neck and jumped off the floor, wrapping her legs around my waist, pushing her hot crotch against my far-too-tight-now jeans. I nearly toppled at the surprise weight but was strong enough to keep my balance as I found my mouth filled with her hard nipple and soft breast.

A happy moan escaped from both of our mouths and I lost my will to deny her, to deny us, any longer. With her legs wrapped tight around me she rubbed her panty covered pussy against my jean-covered cock. She hung with one hand around my neck and used her other to reach down and massage and squeeze the breast I wasn't furiously sucking and nibbling at.

This girl was driving me up the wall. Her enthusiasm and lack of fear to both take what she wanted and to pleasure herself made my heart beat fast as a *Rush* track and my breath to collapse into animal pants.

With my jeans about to explode and every inch of me aching to be closer to her there was no more time to waste. I needed my cock in her. *Now.*

Lucy

He released my breast from his mouth and I let out a little sigh. Two strong hands grabbed me under my arms and he yanked me off his hips as I released my legs.

He took a step forward and then tossed me. I gasped as I flew through the air, momentarily afraid, until I landed on the soft, massive bed behind me with a whoomph as the expensive sheets and comforters deflated.

"Are you going to fuck me now?" I asked him as he strode toward me.

He didn't reply but simply started removing his clothes. I took that as a yes and quickly unzipped my boots and kicked them off, before wriggling out of my remaining clothes.

I bit my lip as I looked at him, now shirtless, before me. Without realising it my left hand started squeezing a breast while my right slipped down between my thighs.

I was naked on the bed, bare to his gaze, as I let my fingers slide between my wet folds while I watched him take off his jeans. He paused a moment, his eyes wide with a wild look on them as he realised I was naked and fingering myself on the bed.

"Never seen a girl touch herself before?"

"Not like that," he said, as he lowered his jeans to the floor, apparently unable to take his eyes off me.

I arched my back and let out a loud moan before withdrawing my fingers and raising them to my lips.

"Oh my God," he said, as I slipped a finger into my mouth, tasting how hot I was for him. "You are something else."

My eyes lowered down his body. "Oh my God, yourself," I said, blinking and suddenly feeling twice as turned on as before, if that was possible.

He'd removed his underwear and revealed the closest thing to a perfect cock I'd ever seen. Big, long, thick, straight and so, so, fucking hard. I guess I could take part of the credit for the final part, but holy shit, as soon as I saw it I knew I needed it. I knew I needed to make it *mine*. And fast.

He grinned. "You like this?" he said, reaching down and holding it by the base, causing it to twitch as if it were hungry. Hungry for me. Hungry to force its way between my legs, deep, deep inside me.

"I like it," I said as I slid two fingers slowly in and out, "I love it." I let out a moan. "I need it."

I let my hands stop pleasuring me as I pulled my knees up and grabbed my ankles, spreading my legs apart, revealing my pussy and ass for him. I know some girls are shy. Not me. If I'm already naked with a guy what the hell left is there to be shy about? Embrace your femininity, your nakedness, your glorious, glorious body, that's what I say.

"Can you take it all?" he asked as he stepped toward the edge of the bed. "Some girls can't."

I felt so open, so vulnerable, so ready for him. Aching. Aching with a need for a hot, hard, *big* cock inside me. "Make me," I said, squirming on the bed. "Make me take it all."

He got onto the bed, up on his knees, towering above me; delicious six pack and rock-carved-chest kneeling between my legs. I felt so small and helpless under him and let out a shiver of anticipation.

His cock seemed to be shaking in anticipation as he grabbed me under my knees and lifted my ass slightly off the bed, and leaned in, his hard cock at my wet pussy entrance.

"Now I'm going to fuck you. You're horny, aren't you? You need it, don't you? You're hungry for my cock, aren't you?"

I bit my lip and moaned and nodded. "Now," I said, "Now. Put it in me now. All of it. I need you to fuck me. I need it."

He pushed the tip of the head against my entrance. It felt so hot the mere touch of it elicited another gasp from me. Would it fit, I wondered? I didn't care; he'd make it fit.

I wrapped my legs around his waist and he reached under me and grabbed my shoulders from behind as he began to plunge his massive cock into my small, tight body.

I let out a loud gasp. "Fuck!"

A brief look of doubt crossed his face but he

continued his remorseless entrance into me. Would it all fit? Could it? My eyes flickered down to my belly; surely it was going to end up half in my stomach.

"Fuck, you're tight," he said as he pushed in further. "Oh fuck. Oh fuck that feels good."

I let out a squeal, my body wracked by conflict, unsure if I was experiencing pain or pleasure. As I was seemingly torn open by his massive cock my body quivered with pleasure mixed in with the pain. Oh shit. It felt like I'd never had sex before; like it was the first time again. How was that possible?

His fingers dug into the top of my shoulders to hold me in place as he gave a final shove of his hips and I let out another yelp. My legs were wrapped tight around him, but that didn't stop my thighs, and the rest of my body, from quivering.

I arched my back and let out a long gasping breath and I felt myself relax, just a touch, the pain of him stretching me disappearing.

"Do it." I said. "Do it to me. Fuck me."

"Hard?" he asked as he slowly withdrew and then thrust back inside me firmly, sending a mini-quake through my body.

I could only speak while he was pulling. When he pushed in again it seemed to snatch my voice out of my throat and only left me with the ability to squeal or snort or gasp or moan; more animal than girl.

"Hard! There will be time later for — " I was going to say something about long, slow sex, but he rammed back into me hard.

"Shit. You're tight. So, so, tight. I won't—" he let out a yelp as I dug my nails into his back. "Last long." He let out a groan as I pulled him even tighter into me with my calves and ankles. "This time."

As he drove into me I flexed my hips, matching his rhythm. I didn't *want* him to last long this time. I wanted a good, hard, fast, fuck. Slow romantic fucking isn't for the first time when you have animal attraction like this.

Now was a time for the frantic fucking of two people in their prime of their lives desperate to make their bodies one.

I grabbed the back of his head and forced his hot lips back down onto mine. I wanted every part of him in me that I could get. He responded hungrily, his tongue and mine intertwining as he continued to seemingly try and force me through the bed with the pounding he was giving me.

Every time he pulled I was amazed at just how much of him was leaving me, and then when he pushed back in I couldn't believe how much of him there was to fit in my little body. From top to toe I glowed with heat. I'd never been filled and fucked like this before. It really was like the first time all over again. Like I'd never had sex, just a pale imitation of it. And if you knew the life I'd lived you'd understand how amazing that was. Who the fuck was this man that could make me feel this way?

I sucked on his tongue, and nibbled on his lower lip, yelping each time he thrust into me. I broke the kiss for a moment.

"Harder. Fuck me harder—" *Thrust.* "Cum. I need you to— " *Thrust.* "Fuck me. Oh God, Oh God, I'm—"

He pounded into me like he wanted to hurt me, and it was just how I needed it. So often men have held back, worrying about me too much, not realising that I get off on raw, uncontrolled, violent animal fucking. Not this one.

His left arm continued to dig into my shoulder, no doubt setting me up for a delicious bruise. His right hand let go and instead grabbed a handful of my long, blond hair, yanking it back causing delicious pain. I was completely under his control, his fuck-toy, and there was no escape possible until he'd cum.

My body was a quivering, sweaty mess as both our breathing turned from moaning breaths to rapid frantic pants.

"I'm going to cum," he said as he forced himself harder and deeper into me than he ever had before.

"Fuck, me too. Fuck. Fuck. Fu—"

I let out a shriek as first my pussy started to contract of its own accord, milking his hard dick, and then my entire body collapsed into something between nirvana and a nuclear detonation. My vision went white, my hearing disappeared, my skin went numb and all that was left was an explosion of pure animal pleasure from deep inside that was so intense I forgot who I was.

A million miles away I heard him let out a distant yell as he used my tight young body to bring himself to a climax in a final flurry of thrusts before holding me so tight I was nearly crushed.

His entire weight pushed me down, deep into the bed as his spent body spasmed and twitched above me. I wouldn't be able to walk for a while but I'd regained control of my hands. I ran my fingers down his spine to the muscular curve of his buttocks and back up again to his neck and now damp hair.

Shallow, rapid, panting breaths, twitching bodies and moans of disbelief filled the air. I buried my face in his neck and breathed in deep, inhaling his manly scent, taking it deep inside my body. I knew this was a moment I'd never ever forget.

Who was this British musician who could do that to me? It didn't seem real. All I knew now was that if I wasn't careful I would get addicted to him, and who the hell knows where that could lead.

But among all the things I've been accused of in life, 'careful' is not one of them. Fuck *careful*, I thought, I'm going all in and seeing just where this wild road will lead.

Johnny

The morning after. This is the bit where you feel guilt or regret for what happened the night before. Where you think *well crap, I'm never drinking again. Or is this really what it's like, is this all there is? One night stands and trashy cum-dumpster groupies?*

But this time was different. I was standing in the bathroom after a hot shower and I felt none of those things. Instead of regret I felt excitement. Instead of guilt I felt promise. Instead of shame I felt electricity running through me as I felt more alive than I had in years.

What a night.

Still, it was just a one night stand, right? You don't go on a rock tour of the the U.S motherfuckin' A and pickup the first girl you meet. Hell no. That'd be ridiculous, wouldn't it?

Nope. It was just a fun night, that was all. And there'd be many, many more to come with dozens of the hottest little thangs America could throw at me. We were getting *famous* now and it'd be pussy-on-tap everywhere we went.

So. It was time to move this one along. *Yeah that was fun, love. See ya around.* That's what I'd do. Too easy.

I checked myself in the mirror. Yep, with the white towel wrapped low around my waist I looked *good*. Give this chick a nice little memory of me to say goodbye.

I took a deep breath and stepped to the bathroom door. As I pulled it open I changed my mind. *One more time, just one more time. Maybe one more day. And then maybe another day. I'm not through with her yet.*

"Babe—" I started to say. Then stopped myself. Because there was no one there. The massive bed looked achingly empty without the nude body that had been lying spreadeagled across it when I'd slipped away for my shower.

"Well, shit."

* * *

Shir-ing, Shi-ring, Shi-ring, I wonder where she

went, Shi-ring, Shi-ring, Shi-ring, God last night was so good, when she put her hands around my cock and teased me by holding the tip against her tongue... shit... Shi-ring... Shi...

I was trying to meditate and it was not going well. It's simple: All I do is repeat my mantra — *Shi-ring* (just 750 pounds from your local maharishi!) — in my head over and over. Boom. Thirty minutes later I feel like a whole new man, mind as empty as my bed was when I'd finished my shower that morning, spirit as clean as my body was, and a general feeling of calm and contentment.

The only problem was, I just couldn't do it today. My mind kept going back to her, that girl, *Lucy*. It was like she'd climbed into my brain and wouldn't get out. She was locked inside my head and she wasn't taking it calmly - she was kicking shit around in there and my attempts at clearing my mind through meditation were failing desperately.

She's only a groupie, I told myself. But it was no good. I'm too dumb to be able to lie to myself effectively. (Or too smart?) For a start, she wasn't a proper groupie (Thanks Matt aka Lonnie! Asshole!), and second she wasn't, *couldn't*, be an 'only' anything. There was something special about her; unique. In a field of flowers she was a fuckin' firework blowing everyone else away in an explosion of weak fluttering petals.

Shit, what's wrong with me? My mind and body were acting like those of a love-struck teenager instead of an adult. In fact, had I ever felt like this about somebody? Maybe with my first girlfriend, Mandy, but that seemed different somehow, and so, so, long ago.

Maybe I need to see a psychologist I thought.

But nope, that wasn't it either.

I knew what the problem was.

Somehow that little American college girl had bollocksed up the wiring in my head. And I was in love.

Love.

I moaned.

That's all I fucking needed right at the beginning of our first fuckin' tour in America.

Lucy

Wow. This place was a mess, I thought, as I scanned up and down the hallway. It was littered with all kinds of crap from beer cans to pizza to even a giant, green, watermelon.

Seems like I'd missed quite the party. Still, I'd had quite the party of my own with the kissable, touchable and oh-so-lickable rockstar. I stretched up to the ceiling and let my arms falls back to my side.

"Hey!" whisper-shouted a familiar voice.

I span around and grinned. There she was. Peeking out of one of the doors was Nicole.

I made me way over, avoiding most of the trash on the floor. As I reached the door I heard the elevator ding and instinctively looked over.

Two men in suits got out. Neither looked very pleased. I recognised one from the very same elevator the night before who Johnny had teased. He looked very, very unhappy. The other man had the same managerial look to him but with more of a presence about him. I guessed he was the superior.

I reached Nicole and squeezed her hand, giving a nod of my head in their direction. I was curious. We both peeked down the hallway at the two men.

"What the fuck has happened to my hotel, Jerry?"

"I tried to stop them. What could I do?"

"What could you do, Jerry? What could you, do? You had a twelve hour shift. Here's a too-late plan of fucking action for you: You could *not* let these assholes do twelve-hundred-fucking-thousand-dollars worth of damage in your twelve hour shift. How about that, huh?"

The poor manager from the night before just stood there, shaking his head. He had nothing to say in his defence. It seemed a little unfair to be blaming him though. Whoever thought it was a good idea to accept a booking from a bunch of rockstars and bikers was to blame really, weren't they?

"Come on," said Nicole as she yanked me into the room.

Although smaller than the room I'd been in the

night before it was still nice; you could see why this hotel was labeled a luxury hotel. And, unlike the hallway, it was in remarkably good condition.

"So! Come on!" she said as she collapsed on to the bed.

I made my way to a leather sofa and let myself sink into it. For a moment I wondered why my body was aching in mysterious places before flashes of the dirty, dirty, but oh-so-good things we'd done to each other returned.

"What?" I asked her.

"Tell me!"

I blinked. "Tell you what?"

She tilted her head and looked at me like there was something wrong with me. Of course there are all kinds of things wrong with me, but this was a look like it was a *new* thing wrong with me.

"Everything! There's something strange about you today Lucy."

"Oh, it was, you know, awesome?" I said.

She shook her head at me. "That's it? Normally I have to stop you from telling me way too many gross personal details. You're usually bursting with things to tell me and you don't spare *any*thing. Today all I get is *awesome*? What the hell happened?"

I put my feet up on the sofa and lowered my head to the armrest. "Well, maybe you're right, maybe I *do* say too much usually."

She gave me a look like I was a puzzle she was trying to figure out. Ain't no one ever going to figure out the puzzle that is Lucy Bennigan though. Well, not all of it, anyway.

"Oh, I get it." She had a knowing smile on her face. "He made you sign an NDA, didn't he?"

I snorted. "A Non-Disclosure Agreement? Him? Umm *The Full Force* isn't that big yet, doofus."

"Oh shit."

I opened my eyes, suddenly worried. "What?"

"I know what's up."

I tilted my head at her.

"You've fallen in love with him! That's why you're being all secret-squirrel about him."

"What? Hell no!" I sat up and put on my stern face. "I do *not* fall in love just like that. In fact, I don't *fall in love.* I fall in temporary lust. You know that. I like to have fun, dammit. I don't get tied down by silly little emotions like love." The more I spoke the less convinced I was.

"Bullshit. You just never found anyone you dug that much."

"I…" I didn't complete my sentence. Was there some truth to the nonsense she was saying? Surely it was ridiculous. You couldn't fall in love after one night, could you? All those movies and books about love at first sight were just bullshit. Everyone knows that. And anyway, it wasn't as simple as that for me.

"You're in lo-ove," she teased.

"Am not. And anyway, you know no *one* man could ever satisfy me."

She shook her head and grinned. "Whatever, hon."

"No, it's true. I told you before, I need two men to make me happy."

She rolled her eyes and shook her head at me. She never believed me when I explained it to her, but I was adamant. I was just wired different to everyone else.

Our discussion was interrupted when the bathroom door opened and Nicole's personal 6-foot-something of yumminess stepped out clad only in a white fluffy towel which seemed to be tantalisingly loose.

He glanced at me on the sofa and for a split second I could see that he was disappointed I was there. Oops.

"Sweetness, why don't you go see if you can rustle up some breakfast for us? I don't think I'll fit in downstairs in their fancy-ass dining room."

"Sure thing." She turned to me. "Coming?"

I shrugged my shoulders. "Sure."

* * *

A cream cheese bagel, a Boston cream, and a large black coffee. What a healthy breakfast, right? With the amount of calories I'd burned off the night before I needed it though.

Nicole wiped powdered sugar from the corner of her mouth and gave me one of her serious looks. Uhoh. It was Spanish Inquisition time I guessed.

"So why'd you sneak out on him then?"

I shrugged my shoulders. "You know, it's all part of the game."

"The game, huh?"

"Yeah. Leave 'em wanting more, right?"

She shook her head at me. "Nope."

I spoke through a mouthful of creamy donut goodness. "What do you mean, 'nope'?"

A sip of coffee before she responded. "You're scared."

I nearly spat out my own coffee at that pronouncement. "Scared? Scared? Me?" I said incredulously, "You know I don't get scared. *Especially* not from guys. Who do you think this is you're talking to?"

A knowing smile and a shake of the head. Infuriating. "You're scared you like him too much. I can see it in your eyes."

"In my eyes?"

"Yep. And on your lips."

"My *lips?*"

She nodded while pointing the remains of a donut at me. "Yep, you keep zoning out with a stupid little smile on your face. I've never seen you do that before."

I shook my head adamantly. "No way."

She nodded. "Yes way, sweet-cheeks."

"Alright, alright. I admit it. I had the time of my goddamn life with him last night. Still, let me play this my way, ok?"

She shrugged. "Sure. If you say so. So, what's 'your way' then?"

"He's a rockstar. On tour. That means fans and groupies and all kinds of women throwing themselves at him, right?"

"Like you," she said with a grin.

I tossed a balled up napkin at her head which she swatted out the way. "Fuck off."

"Just sayin'…"

"Well, let's just see what he does. If he likes me, then he won't be off with other girls, right? And if I was just a fling, well, at least I had one night of fun and didn't get hurt."

"So this is like some retro-active 'hard to get' move? Let him have it, then disappear and see if he still wants it?"

"Stop making it sound stupid. It's a solid plan!"

She shook her head at me and grinned. "You crack me up Lucy. I never know what the hell you're going to do next."

We grabbed hands across the table. "That's why you love me, right?"

"I guess so," she said shaking her head and laughing.

We sat in friendly silence sipping our coffees. It wasn't just him I was worried about. It was me. I was scared of the crazy feelings I'd experienced the night before. I don't subscribe to the idea of love at first sight, instalove, bullshit. So what the hell was wrong with me?

I needed a time-out from him. And shit, I still had next semester's tuition to worry about. I gulped down the last of my coffee.

"Let's go. I gotta find a computer."

"A computer?" asked Nicole.

"Yeah. Got some research to do."

She shook her head again in bemusement. I gave myself a secret smile. She'd flip when she found out what it was I was researching, and that *she'd* be helping me with it later.

Johnny

"Well shit, don't look like that. Come with me. If Chad Chad Price knows one thing, it's exactly what you need. Trust me."

I looked up at our manager from the table I was sitting at in the dingy hotel bar that didn't look like it had been updated since it first opened in the 50s. Everyone else had fucked off somewhere or other. I was hanging about, like an idiot, hoping *she* would show. She didn't.

It'd been a crap day all round. First, she'd disappeared. Then I find my band and Matt aka Lonnie's friends had trashed the hotel. Then, get this, the cops roll up with the manager. Boom. We're kicked the hell out. That's why I was now in this craphole of a bar in this dilapidated excuse for a hotel.

It's hard to feel very rock'n'roll in a run down old place. Even the screaming fans who'd been outside the luxury hotel we'd spent the first night in were gone. I wasn't sure whether it was because they hadn't found us yet, or whether they wrinkled up their noses at the thought of waiting outside this flea-bitten old dive.

And then there was the show. The show sucked. Except for me the band were all still fucked up from the night before. Then, get this, some asshole pulled Neal, my lead guitarist off the stage. Prick ended up with a broken jaw, but still, it wasn't what was supposed to be happening on the second night of our tour.

"How do you know what I need?" I asked Chad.

"Well I know what anyone would need after what I'm about to tell you. Hard liquor." He leaned in close. "And a better place than here to drink it."

I raised my eyebrows at him. Chad Chad Price was the annoying man with the annoying name who was supposedly going to make us big in America. 5'6" of used car salesman grease-ball and overconfident twattishness. But he guaranteed he'd make us big in the US, and if he could do that, well, I'd put up with all his greasiness, swagger, and more. "What the fuck else could go wrong?"

He sighed. "Si. Your bassist—"

"I know who my fucking bassist is."

"He's gone."

I looked up from my bottle of beer. I hadn't been expecting *that*. "What do you mean 'gone'?"

"Gone. Left. Disappeared. Absent Without Leave, vamoosed, or, as you lime-eating Queen-lovers would say, buggered off."

I shook my head. This didn't make any sense at all. What was going on? "Have you called him? You sure he's gone? The fuck am I going to do without a bassist?"

"Phone's off. His letter said don't bother trying to find him. Trust me, he's fuckin' gone," Chad Chad said. He leaned down toward me at the table, speaking more quietly like he was revealing a massive secret. "But worry not. You've got Chad Chad Price on your team. I've got this."

"You've got this? What does that mean?"

He nodded. "Got six bassists coming in the morning to audition. Session musicians. And your man Lonnie is on the case tracking Si's ass down."

"Six bassists tomorrow? What? How? How

long's he been missing? Fuck. I don't understand what the hell is going on, Chad."

He flashed a brilliant white smile at me. "Worry not. Now come with me. We're going to go relieve our stresses."

I shook my head. "No thanks."

He slammed his hands on the table. "Get the fuck up, pussy. I thought you Brits were supposed to be tough. You're not going to let a little American like me out-do you, are you?"

Huh. That was fighting talk. "Alright, alright. Arsehole. Where're we going?"

He flashed a grin of victory. "You'll see."

And so with that, I followed Chad Chad Price, so much of a twat they named him twice, out of the bar to fuck-knows-where. My mind was like a fucked-up blender filled with churning thoughts of Lucy and my band on the verge of collapse without Si, my apparently missing friend and bassist.

I should probably go to my room and meditate, do a yoga session, and get some sleep, I thought. But shit, sometimes the allure of some hard liquor and some banter wins out. Especially when you've had a day as terrible as I had.

So against my better judgment I followed Chad outside into the surprisingly warm LA darkness and whatever mischief he had lined up for us.

Lucy

"You've to be kidding me," said Nicole.

I grabbed her right hand in both of mine, squeezed it tight and pulled her toward me. "*Please?*" I fake-whined. "We're here now. What's the harm?"

Her eyes flashed up to the sign and down again and I knew I'd won. I knew I'd win anyway, I always do with her. She just gets to apply the brakes a little bit, but we always end up doing what I suggest.

The place looked gloriously sleazy. A real dive. The facade was lit up with a neon silhouette of a nude woman sitting down, knees drawn up but with one leg kicking out provocatively. To the left of that was a large neon arrow with a sign reading *Topless Women* indicating toward the door.

"Okay, okay. Let's just have a look," said Nicole with a sigh, "I guess I've always been curious."

I grinned at her and released her hand before thumping her on the arm.

"Ow!"

I giggled. "Look!" I pointed at another temporary sign lit up by a floodlight. It read *Now Hiring Class of 2015.*

"This place is *so* sleazy," said Nicole shaking her head in disgust.

"Yeah, it's great, isn't it?" I said defeating her mock disgust with my enthusiasm. "Come on!"

We went through the entranceway and had to make an immediate turn. There was a doorman there, a big grizzly kind of guy with an ex-military vibe who looked like he'd been working the door since 'Nam. he reminded me of an older chubbier version of Gauge, the Sons of Mayhem's own hard-as-nails military veteran.

"Auditions are in the afternoon," he growled, "come back between 2 and 5. Larry'll sort you out."

Nicole tugged at my arm like she wanted to leave already, before we'd even had any fun. I really couldn't figure out how her mind worked sometimes. Any of the time. And not just her, most other people. Maybe *I* was the weird one? Nah…

"We're not here to audition," I said, "There're

83

girls in there, right?"

"Yeah…" he answered slowly, squinting at us, "there's girls. That's why you're here?"

I nodded firmly while Nicole let out another of her infamous sighs. "Damn right that's why we're here. How much to get in?"

"Entry's free. Two drink minimum. And don't forget to tip."

The bouncer stepped to the side to let us in. I marched down the hallway with Nicole in tow.

"Have fun!" yelled the doorman as we left.

"Always do!" I yelled back.

We approached a set of twin doors, behind which music could be heard booming out. Would this be music I'd be dancing to in the future, I wondered? Would this be what paid for my college tuition?

Before I could push open the doors and lead us in Nicole grabbed me again.

"What exactly are we going to do here?"

I gave her a sly smile. "We'll get some drinks. Admire the girls, and…"

"And?" she asked with a frown.

"And get a lap dance."

"*Really?* I don't want to say that."

I nodded confidently. "Of course. I need to see how it's done, right? And anyway, I want to talk to a couple of the girls. Get the inside scoop, y'know?"

"Why don't you just slip a girl a few bucks and ask her some questions instead?" She let out a sigh."Whatever. You owe me though."

I squeezed her arm. "I'll get you back, don't worry." I paused a beat. "I'll buy *you* a lap dance!"

"Hey!" She went to punch my arm but I slipped out the way, grabbed her hand, and led her inside, the dim lights and throbbing music seeming to swallow us whole as we entered.

Johnny

"A strip club? Are you kidding me?" I asked. We were outside a large neon lit building with an array of sleazy signs strung up outside.

"What? You don't like women? Want me to take you to a gay strip club instead?" asked Chad.

"No, of course not! I love women! But—"

He shook his head and gave a knowing smile. "So no problem then, right?"

I gave a dejected shrug. "I'm supposed to be a rock star, banging groupies, not heading out to pay for the questionable pleasure of some crack head strippers."

"Yeah, well, trust me, these girls are much more fun." He started in through the door and turned to look at me. "Anyway, some of them are coke-heads not crack-heads."

Man this guy was fucked. How had we ended up with *him* as a manager I asked myself for the hundredth time since our Virgin Atlantic jet had landed at sunny

LAX.

I followed him inside past a grizzled old bouncer as big as an old fashioned red telephone box who gave Chad a high five as we entered. It was more of a low five for the doorman though. They obviously knew each other. I guessed Chad was a regular and shuddered at the thought.

A few minutes later we were sat a short distance from the stage where a dark skinned girl with what looked like prison tats was swinging around a stripper pole. I couldn't imagine how strong their legs and bodies must be to keep them held out like that. I do yoga so I know a thing or two about flexibility and core strength, but there was no way I could have hung from the pole like this chick was doing.

"Nice, huh?" said Chad giving me a jab on the arm with the bottom of his bottle of beer.

"Yeah. Great, Chad. Really great. When I dreamed, as a young lad, of being a rockstar in America this is exactly what I imagined it'd be like. Sitting in a dingy strip club with a greasy little shite while an escaped convict dances on a pole for our edification.

Spot on, Chad."

"Are you not happy, Johnny? Something got you down?"

I shook my head uncomprehendingly at the moron. Had he forgotten already that I'd just lost my bassist, I wondered. He didn't know about Lucy of course, but surely my band disintegrating right before my very eyes was enough to get me down, right?

"What do you think?"

He unscrewed the cap of Maker's Mark he had in front of him and poured two good sized glasses. What better to go with a bottle of beer than a warm half pint of bourbon, eh?

"It's all part of the game, son. And let me tell you a little secret..."

I took a burning gulp of the bourbon before mouthing out "*What?*" to him, my voice temporarily snatched away by the liquor.

"It's a good thing. Your boy running away."

I looked at the bottle of bourbon and then back at Chad. Had he somehow teleported a bunch of it into his brain and scrambled it already, I wondered. How on earth could Si running away be a good thing.

"It's all about marketing," he continued.

"Marketing?"

Chad took another big gulp of the liquor followed by a swig of beer. "Yep. Marketing. *Viral* marketing. Social media. All that shizznat."

"Marketing ain't gonna' play bass guitar, buddy."

Chad grinned. "Fuck the bass guitar. Fuck your bassist. This is news, Johnny, *news!* Runaway rockstars are *awesome.*" He put down his drinks and grabbed me by the shoulders, shaking them, "every disaster you have makes the news and builds buzz. Getting kicked out of the hotel today? That, too, was awesome! We're making you stars, Johnny, *stars!* Why the hell do you think I allowed your biker friend to run security for you guys? Because it's bound to make yet more headlines, buddy!*"

"Really? That's how you make stars? Losing half the band and getting us kicked out of hotels? I know showbiz in America is fucked, just like back home, but really man?"

He took another drink. "Really buddy. Now tell

me about this girl."

I cocked my head at him. That question came out of nowhere. "What girl?"

"What girl? What girl? You forgotten her already? The one you were carrying around with her ass on show yesterday."

"Oh, that girl?"

"*That* girl? You've had others already, huh, well you've been a busy boy haven't you."

"No, there were no others. Just her."

"Was she as wild as she looked? She came along with the bikers. You best hope she isn't one of their old ladies." He paused as if thinking a moment. "Actually, it'd be *great* if it was one of their old ladies. Imagine the news stories after you get hospitalized by your own security…"

I gulped. Shit, she wasn't anyone's old lady was she? She sure as shit better not be. I thought for a second or two then breathed deep. Panic averted. There was no way she was the cheating type - she might like to have fun, but I could tell she was loyal at least.

"Look, Chad, one, you are *not* to get me, or

anyone else in my band, hospitalized. Two, she is no one's old lady. You got that?"

He laughed. "Shame." He turned his head to look at the stage. "Look at the thighs on that," he said shaking his head in disbelief, now this one has got some class to her.

I gulped down the rest of the bourbon in my glass, poured another, leaned back in my seat and turned to watch the stage. Figured I might as well try and get *some* enjoyment out of this sleazehole.

The previous girl had gone and been replaced, and goddamn this girl had a body on her. She was facing away from me, blond hair hanging down her back covering the strap of her bra, but she was exactly my type. In fact, she reminded me of...

I spat out my drink. "What the fuck!"

Chad cocked his head at me. "Banging bod, right?"

The girl had turned around and as she did our eyes locked.

It was her.

The girl from last night.

Lucy.

Lucy

Nicole gave me a little frown as I beckoned the girl over. The stripper was Asian with big oval eyes and several tattoos on her honey-colored arms. She was dressed in *fuck-me* boots, tiny boy-shorts that had the top-button undone and you knew could be dropped provocatively in an instant. The little shorts didn't quite cover the top string of a thong. On top she was wearing a push-up bra that gave her a surprisingly cavernous amount of cleavage considering her small size.

She tilted her head at us questioningly as she arrived at our dilapidated little wooden table, a pitcher of beer placed between us.

"What do you want?" she said loudly with a thick accent. The questioning look in her eyes didn't indicate hostility, it seemed that her blunt question was due to the fact she had pretty limited English and was trying to be heard over the music.

"You wanna lapdance?" She fingered the top of

her tiny shorts as she spoke, revealing more of her honey skin underneath and the promise that they would soon disappear.

I opened my mouth to answer *yes*. After all, I've got to study this stuff, right?

"No," said Nicole before I could speak. "She wants to ask you some questions is all."

I kicked her under the table. She kicked me back, harder. I grinned. Nicole was still so uptight about stuff. Still, Nicole was probably right. I bet I could learn more from talking to her instead of just watching her give a lapdance.

"Can you sit down a minute?" I asked

"Twenty dollars," she said by way of a reply, leaning in toward me.

I sighed and pulled a twenty out of the far-too-thin stack I had in my purse. I needed to start earning some cheddar. And fast. I handed it over with a grimace and then she did something I didn't expect.

Instead of pulling up a chair as I thought she would she simply straddled my leg, her soft smooth skin pressed up against mine as her citrusy perfume flooded over me. She wrapped an arm sensuously around my neck. I felt myself beginning to flush. Looking across the table I saw Nicole looking at me wide-eyed and with cheeks more crimson than mine.

Since shocking my darling-yet-reserved friend is one of my dearest hobbies I decided to let the girl stay where she was, and wrapped my arm around her waist. Her skin was warm and soft but taut over her flat stomach, with little fat covering her.

Don't get me wrong, I'm not really into girls — give me a nice muscular man, or better yet, *two*, any day — but I could still appreciate the primal sexiness she gave off. I bet she earned some great tips from the guy customers.

"How're you doing?" I asked her for want of a better question.

"I'm fine, thank you," she said, biting her lip and looking way too deep into my eyes. I wondered whether it was an act — her just doing what she normally did with the men — or whether she actually *was* flirting with me. I grinned. *I wouldn't blame her, I am pretty hot.* There's a fine line between arrogance and self-confidence, but I'm pretty sure I'm still on the good side of it. Right?

"So what you wanna' know?" she finally asked me, her plumped up lips getting the sounds of the words just a little wrong in her Asian accent.

Her body was hot against mine and I felt the skin of my leg becoming damp where she rested, her body seemingly feather-light as she pressed against me.

"Sorry, but it's a little personal." I said, biting my lip in embarrassment.

She reached forward and brushed a loose hair out of my eyes with long, red nails and lifted her eyebrows in a question. A *suggestive* question.

I giggled. "Not that kind of personal. I mean, it's about money."

She raised her eyebrows even further and her hand caressed my face, as she gave me a curious look. She really was getting all the wrong ideas.

We were speaking quietly enough that Nicole couldn't hear us on the other side of the table over the music. I could see her staring at us wondering what we were saying.

"I don't mean that," I said giggling as I gently lowered the hand from my face.

A disappointed yet mischievous frown crossed her face and she interlinked her tiny fingers with mine, resting our hands on top of her smooth thigh.

"I mean, I was thinking of working in a place like this." I jerked my head to indicate the room. "You know, to earn some money."

The girl's face opened in toothy grin and I felt her quake on my leg and through the palm of my hand as she gave a little giggle.

"You wanta' dance?"

I nodded at her. "Maybe. But, I want to know if it's worth it, you know? How much can you make? I need to pay for college."

She nodded in understanding. "Yeah, you can pay for college. If you can do it. If the guys like you." She ran a hand up my arm. "I think they'll like *you*." She grinned.

"Oh yeah?" I said with a smile at the thought of my money problems being over. "I can do it. It wouldn't be here though," I said waving my arm around the dingy club, "We don't live around here. Just on vacation."

The girl let out a laugh and smacked me on the arm. She threw out an arm to indicate the room. "Shitty vacation," she said in loud amusement.

She leaned in close and another wave of her perfume washed over me. I bet she made loads of money here, I thought. She exuded a promise of sensuality with every movement and I doubt any man who came to a place like this would be able to resist her allure for long. "You wanna try?"

I raised my eyebrows at her. I almost *did* want to try.

She smacked me on the arm. "Dancing," she said.

I giggled. Oops.

"My set next. You try after?" she asked in her somewhat broken and accented English.

"Sure, why not," I said with a shrug of my shoulders and surge of excitement. There's a first time for everything, right? "By the way, my name's Lucy."

She leaned in and spoke into my air, hot breath tickling, "You, me."

I jerked my head back and looked at her in confusion.

She frowned and smacked my arm. Again. "My name. Yumi. Come on." She slipped off my leg like a butterfly alighting from a leaf and pulled me to my feet.

Nicole gave me a what-the-fuck look as I leaned across the table. "Wanna' dance with me?" I said, indicating the stage with a grin and a flick of my hair.

She shook her head in a kind of awed amazement at me. "No thanks. I'm good here. I thought they only did auditions in the day time?"

I frowned at her. "Baby," I said pushing out my chest and running a hand down my body. "A body this fine don't need no audition."

I felt someone swat my ass, hard, and my head swiveled around sharply as I looked for someone to smack. Instead all I saw was Yumi laughing at me. She squeezed the hand she still held.

I turned back to see Nicole laughing at me too. I shrugged my shoulders and grinned.

"Come on!" said Yumi excitedly.

"Nice tattoo by the way," said Nicole to Yumi.

I turned to look at what she meant. On the young girl's shoulder was a tattoo of a man in a white lab coat, eyes bulging out, hanging from a noose with a red x next to him.

I gave Nicole a quizzical look, it was a little morbid for her, I thought. Yumi was already pulling me away before I could figure out what she meant.

"Thanks!" yelled my new companion over her shoulder as she led me across the floor.

I heard a couple of wolf whistles just before we reached the dancers' entrance. We both turned around to smile flirtatiously at the source of the whistle, a friendly looking older man in an training suit. Pure class.

Yumi wrapped her hand around my waist, giving me a squeeze. "Come on. Let's give you sexy clothes!"

I laughed and let her guide me through the door. This might be fun, I thought.

Lucy

After she'd given me something even more revealing to wear I watched her from the side of the stage. She moved like a snake, flexing and stretching every which way as she moved in time to the music that flowed through the air. She ran a hand up between her legs and opened her mouth in an O of pleasure. Faked or not, this girl knew what she was doing.

I can do this, I thought to myself.

I watched in envy as $1, $5 and even $10 bills were slipped into her g-string. She must clean up. How much could she make in a night? Five hundred bucks? Shit, with a job like that it wouldn't take me long to earn the tuition I needed for next semester. The semester I didn't want to be doing in the first place. The semester I shouldn't *have* to do, but which I would need since the summer class that would have allowed me to graduate early had been cancelled.

She wasn't up there long, maybe three songs, but

during her dance she had to subtly deposit wads of cash into the waiting hands of one of the other dancers who sat by the side, holding it for her.

Finally she came back, her body shiny and slick with both oil and sweat. She gave me a wild grin and a hug, pushing bare breasts into my bikini covered bosom in a gesture of support.

"Still wanna try?" she asked, her voice slightly panting from the dancing.

I gulped. "Sure!" I said with a bit more enthusiasm than I actually felt, hiding my trepidation. I guessed *everyone* was somewhat nervous before they did this for the first time, right?

But fuck it. You only live once, and hey, even if I didn't end up in this line of work, at least it's an experience, right? Something to tell the grandkids. Well, maybe... We'll see how cool they are.

A new song came on and I felt a little surge inside. It was the Beyonce number that I had jokingly played when I pretended I was going to strip for Nicole. My jam. I knew it like the back of my hand and had even practiced some moves.

I stalked off the side of the stage toward the center and I could see the look of surprise on Yumi's face at my confidence. It was hard to see the audience because of the way the lighting got in my eyes. But that was probably for the best. They'd only make me more nervous if I could actually see them.

"Woo!... Work it!... Shake it!" and other phrases were yelled out at me and a hot rush of confidence soared through my body. I felt hot, flexible, sexy and *invincible*. I couldn't help but smile. I wasn't going to be one of those sultry looking dancers with the sad eyes and pouty lips, I was going to be a happy grinning little sexpot. I hoped.

I was wearing ridiculously high heels and what was basically a tiny bikini. I wasn't wearing a g-string though I guess they could see *most* of my butt nonetheless, and I wasn't going to be taking my top off tonight. No way I'd do that unless I was getting paid properly. It's like a first date, you don't go all the way. *Oh wait, what did I do last night...*

I let my eyes lose focus and ignored the audience as I lost myself in the song.

The sick beat and soaring vocals spirited me away and soon I didn't remember where I was. Sometimes, if the mood is right, music can do that to me. Pull me away from planet earth into some ethereal plane where I just seem to disappear and become one with the beats and melodies.

I've heard that drugs can do that to you too. But I don't need 'em. Not when the mood and the music is right.

I danced across the stage, working my body into one provocative pose after another, flicking my hair, shaking my ass and running my hands all over myself, lost in my moves.

Until something snapped me right the fuck back to reality that is. A hand. A hand slipping *under* the waistband of my bikini. I panicked and snapped up straight and took account of my situation. I realized I'd been facing away from the audience, my hands down around my ankles as I worked my rear end right up against the edge of the stage.

Someone had taken the opportunity to slip their hand into my bikini bottom and sent me into a panic.

Shit.

I span around, eyes wide and glaring, but luckily at the same time as a beat hit so it looked like it was part of a routine. In my sudden rage I was ready to put my heel in the face of whoever it was copping a feel. As I whipped around I felt something scratchy around my waist.

I glanced down and to my surprise saw a dollar bill poking out of the waist. *Ah.* That's what it was. What was wrong with me? Wasn't that the *point* of being up there dancing?

I stepped back, shaking my hips as I did so, knowing I was losing it. I'd left the Starship Music and was back on planet earth and the reality of what I was doing sunk in.

What the fuck was I thinking, dancing on a stage in someone else's itsy-bitsy bikini so some greasy motherfuckers could slip their hands down and cop a feel while they slipped me a few bucks.

Shit. This wasn't me.

You're a smart girl, Lucy. You don't need to be doing this shit. There's got to be a better way to make the money you need.

The song was nearly over and I figured I'd stay out on the stage, well away from the edge, just until it was over, and then I'd leave it forever. I flicked my head side to side, seeing poles on both sides. I hadn't done anything with the poles because, quite frankly, I didn't know how. I'd briefly considered taking up pole dancing purely as a source of exercise but the closest place had been a forty minute drive away, and who has that kind of gas money to burn? Not me, that's for sure.

I raised my hands up into the air and swayed my hips, stretching my flat stomach like a cat. With the song nearly over I risked another look into the audience, temporarily out of the glare of the spotlights, looking to see if Nicole was watching me. Maybe I could blow her kiss or something to embarrass her. Maybe that'd get my mojo back.

But my eyes didn't find Nicole. "Fuck," I whispered to myself.

My eyes hadn't found my friend. Instead, they had, unbelievably, impossibly, caught those of the man I knew I needed to forget. Johnny. Johnny the freakin' rockstar who'd done things to my quivering body the night before that hadn't seemed possible. Johnny the freakin' rockstar I wasn't going to see again.

His mouth opened and I think mine did too. The song ended and as it did so the club dropped into a sudden silence. The DJ, like me, had fucked up.

"Lucy!?"

My hands dropped to my face in a confused panic and I started to run off the stage, the stupid high heels I was wearing click-clacking the whole way. The room was silent except for a muffled cough and the ridiculously loud noise the shoes made as I fled, red-cheeked.

I heard one last wolf whistle before a record scratching sound filled the air followed by the voice of Kendrick Lamar as the DJ got his shit together and the music returned. Too late to make my embarrassment anything but complete.

Lucy

I walked across the room like it was my job. I wasn't going to act embarrassed, I'd done what I'd done and that was that. If he didn't like it then, well, he could suck my... Damn, there wasn't really a good female equivalent for that expression, was there?

I could see him eyeing me up as I approached him. He had a look in his eye like he wasn't quite sure what to make of me. I couldn't quite tell whether he was angry, amused, or disappointed. Whatever.

Pushing my chest out further and keeping my chin held high I approached him. He was sitting next to his manager, the execrable Chad Chad Price and it looked like they were trying to kill a bottle of bourbon between them.

"Hey Sweet-cheeks, how much for a lapdance?"

"Shut up, Chad," said Johnny much to my relief and amusement. "Come on," he said to me gesturing toward a booth.

I nodded and followed the tall, tatted rocker, curious as to what he was going to say. A muffled sigh escaped from between pursed lips as I eyed his tight, jean-clad ass. Why'd he have to look so damn good? I was definitely going to have to put a stop to whatever it was between him and me before I went and did something stupid like fall for him. Urgh.

I followed him over to the booth where we slid to opposite sides, facing each other. I brushed a strand of blonde hair out of my eyes and waited. Let him speak first.

"So," he said.

So much for waiting for him to speak first.

"So," I replied, looking him over again but this time from the front. Yep, he still looked good despite the lateness of the hour. However much bourbon he'd drunk with Chad it hadn't dulled his eyes at all. In fact they seemed livelier than ever and if I wasn't mistaken there was a glint of a smirk on his face. Asshole.

"I thought you were a student."

"I am. I'm a student who was *supposed* to be graduating this summer." I couldn't help but let a tone of complaint enter my voice. What had happened to me was fucked up and the only person I'd really vented to had been Nicole.

"And," he continued his train of enquiry, "I thought your college was, like, miles from here. I thought you were just on vacation. Watching the band."

"I am."

"Ah. So what's this?" he asked, waving in the general direction of the stage, "A working holiday?"

I giggled. Funny asshole. "No."

"Well then?"

"What's it to you? I was just a lay, right? You've got tons of groupies after you. I saw them outside the hotel last night." He didn't have any right to be questioning me. He had no claim on me. Well, he *had* claimed me last night. But that was just for a night. And it wouldn't be happening again. Probably.

He shrugged. "Yeah. There are a few girls hanging around. But..." his voice trailed off.

"But what?" He didn't want *them*, right. Not after he'd tasted *moi (*French 101 for the win!). But he was too embarrassed to say it.

He shrugged. "Nothing. So how come you're working here?"

I gave him a kick and my shoe slipped off. I left it on the floor.

"I'm *not* working here, I told you already."

"You're *not* working here? You could have fooled me. I mean, correct me if I'm wrong, but didn't I just see you up on the stage in a little bikini?"

"Ummm," I stalled.

"If you're not working, then," he waved a hand in front of his face as if grasping for an explanation, "you're, like, a volunteer?"

"Err..." I stammered. This was *not* like me. But the right way of explaining just what I was doing up on the stage shaking my ass and getting money shoved down my panties just wouldn't come. I've had to explain a lot of things in my life but that wasn't one of them.

"You know," he continued with an irritatingly cute smirk on his face, "*most* volunteers go to like, nursing homes, or hospitals, or pick up rubbish or something. I didn't know you could volunteer as a *stripper*." He looked around the room appraisingly. "Though, I guess quite a few of the people here are quite old. Is that it? Are you on a day trip from the nursing home you're volunteering at?"

I giggled. The asshole was teasing me. But the bastard was making me laugh at the same time. A volunteer stripper...

"No. Shut up a minute. I'll tell you, not that I have to, you know. I don't owe you anything."

He arched his eyebrows, raised the corners of his mouth in an annoyingly infectious grin, and rested his hands on the table near mine. We both leaned in a little and I caught a hint of his cologne, mixed with the sweet smell of bourbon and the heady aroma of eau-de-Johnny.

"Didn't say you did owe me anything. But still, relieve my curiosity at least."

So I told him my sad little tale, of how I was planning to graduate early by taking summer classes, but due to events beyond my control it wasn't going to happen and how I'd be stuck with a stupidly large tuition bill as well. I also let him know there was no way I was taking a loan. Not my style.

While I was speaking he nodded understandingly, his stupidly gorgeous eyes looking into mine, the tiredness almost seeming to drain away as he listened to what must surely have been a rather boring tale.

When I'd finished I realized that something weird had happened and gave a little frown. Without prior thought on my part, somehow, my right hand had ended up enclosed in both of his. His warmth and strength seeming to be flowing into me, reassuring me. That wasn't supposed to be happening.

Hadn't I told Nicole earlier that I definitely wasn't going to see the guy again? And now I was letting him hold my hand.

But, somehow, I was also doing something much worse. I realized that after I'd let my shoe slip off I had absentmindedly run my foot up and down his calf. And now, as he was leaning in across the table at me I became aware of what my traitorous foot was doing: Bizarrely, inexplicably, it had actually slipped all the way up his leg and I now found my big toe pressing against the crotch of his jeans. Jeans that seemed to be emanating heat.

"You know we can't, right?" I said to him.

"No?" he answered, looking at me with his ridiculously smoldering eyes.

His hands left mine and went below the table, grasping me with one hand by the ankle, the other clasping my foot, one thumb pressing against the arch in a kind of massage. He pulled the foot in and deliberately rubbed it against the bulge of his jeans. I could feel his cock through the thick fabric and I couldn't help but wiggle my toes against the outline of his hardness.

"No," I continued, slipping off my other shoe, "I decided. You're too dangerous."

"Me? Dangerous?" he pressed my foot hard against his crotch and rubbed it. He glanced down.

I slipped off my other shoe and placed it in his lap.

"Yeah. Dangerous."

Would he do what I thought he was going to do, I wondered? Would he dare do it, here, in this ratty club? Did he have the balls?

"Yeah. Dangerous for me."

He did. His hands left my feet for a minute and and worked the buttons of his fly, loosening the jeans in what surely must have been some serious relief for him.

"You're dangerous because I can't be with you. And you can't be with me."

He worked his cock out from his underwear under the table and with a thud I felt it smack against the underside of the wooden surface.

Damn, he was hard and I couldn't help myself, I couldn't resist. While my mouth said one thing, and my brain thought one thing, my body acted as if it had a mind of its own. I placed the sensitive soles of my two feet around his hardness, pulling it down slightly away from the table. I saw him bite his lip in a moment of weakness, showing emotion in a most unmanly like way.

"It looks like we're going to be together tonight," he said.

I gently, ever so gently, flexed my ankles, holding his rigid manhood between my feet, sensitive toes curling around his hot, hard cock. Each one of the ten pads of my toes could feel the pulsating rigidness of him and I felt myself getting hot and damp.

"Nuh uh."

I couldn't work it fast, although I was dextrous I wasn't skilled at this. It had been a while since I'd been able to say it was my first time, but this? Giving a hot English rock star a footjob in an LA strip club at which I'd just been dancing? Yeah, it was a first time. I was a veritable virgin of stripclub footjobs.

He wrapped his hands around my feet and began to guide them, jerking himself off but using me to do it.

"You're coming back with me tonight." His voice was stern, but slightly strained.

"Am not." My brain ordered my voice to say it with steely determination. But it didn't come out that way. It came out more like a teasing challenge. Like I didn't mean it at all.

He pumped my feet faster against his cock and he seemed to grow hotter than ever. It was like getting some crazy kind of foot massage while also getting to pleasure a hot guy at the same time. I'd always been sensitive there, but this was a feeling I'd never experienced.

"Yes—" he had to pause for a moment "—you *are*."

"No…." I said biting my lip, "Not today." I was almost moaning as I felt him moving faster and faster.. What was this? *He* was the one who was getting physically pleasured. Why the hell was it turning *me* on so much. I couldn't do anything but go with it. I squeezed my toes and watched his pupils dilate further and what might have been a yelp escape from his lips.

He brought his eyes back down to look into mine.

His voice was hard as he said, "Look, you little cock tease," there's no way I'm going to let *you* do this to *me* without me giving you," he paused to let out a sharp blast of breath as I pressed my toes hard against his firm flesh. "Just... you are coming back to my room tonight."

Him giving me what? I guess he lost his train of thought there. I couldn't blame him, I could hardly keep my own thoughts straight.

He was moving me against him at a frantic pace

now and it was all I could do to maintain my upper body composure. My eyes scanned the room to make sure no one was watching and I caught the eye of Nicole, who was now sitting with Chad, sipping on something. Strangely, Yumi was with them too and seemed to be in street clothes now.

Nicole shook her head at me and grinned. She obviously couldn't see what was going on *under* the table.

I bit my lip as he squeezed my arches tightly around his shaft. God this was so freakin' hot.

"Fuck," he let out quietly as he pumped himself furiously.

I watched wide eyed as he let his head drop back with a thump onto the top of the chair.

BANG. He kicked the underside of my chair and I felt a jolt go right through me. He burst like a rocket and I almost thought I could hear it, even though it was impossible with the noise of the music in the club.

I felt the hard cock between my feet pulse, shooting out streams of his hot, sexy seed onto my calves and toes. I'd never felt anything like it, and coming from him, in the sheer heat of the moment it was one of the most sensual experiences of my life. I felt him slow down, and the last few drops dribbled onto my toes.

"Holy shit," he muttered and reached for a handful of napkins.

I tilted my head at him and grinned.

"Like that?"

He shook his head, not in disagreement, but in awe. *Knew it. Damn I'm good. Even when it's my first time.*

Gentleman that he was, he began to wipe my calves and then feet first, squeezing the tense muscles as he did so and lightly massaging my lower lower legs.

He was working on cleaning himself up when it happened.

When shit hit the fan.

CRASH.

The large bouncer we'd seen on our way in smashed through the doors, almost flying as he was rushed by four thickset, dark haired men in black suits and white shirts.

The bouncer was red-faced and grunting as he tried to grab onto the men around him, arms flailing wildly. They forced him back at speed in a wild rush and as one they picked him up and smashed him down on top of a table.

"What the f—"

Johnny

Have you ever gotten a footjob from a sexy little American college student who definitely *wasn't* working (only volunteering!) in a grimy little stripclub, only to find that upon completion your post-cum-moment-of-bliss was rudely interrupted by four Asian mafiosos intent on a kidnapping? No? Well, it was a first for me too.

I'd just about managed to clean myself up when the door got kicked down by four angry looking men in suits tossing a bouncer like he was a floormat they were rolling out for their own welcome.

"What the fuck!?" said Lucy.

I would have said the same thing if she hadn't already beaten me to it.

"Never a dull moment in the States, is there?" I said instead.

She tilted her head at me and frowned.

While I rapidly re-inserted my todger back into

my underpants and jeans the four besuited gangsters left the gasping, moaning and barely conscious bouncer lying in the shattered remains of a table and marched at speed in a tight group across the room on a mission of their own.

Looking around the room it was clear no one was planning on stopping them from whatever it was they were intending on doing. I could see some kind of manager guy staring wide eyed from behind the bar, and next to him a single other bouncer who wasn't making any kind of move. I guessed they didn't plan on having to repel an invasion on a quiet night like this.

"Oh, shit! Yumi!" said Lucy.

Why? *Oh, shit* indeed. They were heading right for the table at which sat her friend, my manager and some other stripper — Yumi?. Another volunteer, perhaps?

"Come on!" she said as she smacked my shoulder while I did up the last button on my fly.

Really? Damnit. She was already getting up and scampering barefoot across the floor.

I scrambled to my feet, belt still undone and

dangling and headed after her. I wasn't looking forward to our arrival. If there's anything I've learned about fighting in my many years of hanging around the bad part of town it's that firstly, avoid it like the plague, and secondly don't ever, ever, ever fight if you're outnumbered. In real life you ain't going to Bruce Lee a whole pack of guys — you're just going to get turned into minced meat.

Oof, I thought as I watched the action begin in earnest. The leading man grabbed Chad by the scruff of his neck and tossed him away like he was a small sack of potatoes.

"Fuck you!" Chad managed to get out as he flew through the air before landing on his back onto a table which *didn't* collapse, inches from a topless dancer who had been giving a lapdance before the invasion began, and was now cuddling up to her client more in fear than affection.

I hurried after Lucy fast, not really looking forward to arriving.

Two of the men grabbed Yumi, one arm each, and lifted her bodily into the air.

She wasn't going down without a fight though and as they lifted her up she used the strength of her dancer's body to snap at the waist, swinging up her hips and a black booted leg. Using her momentum she kicked wildly at the face of one of the other two men, catching him right in the eye with the pointed heel of her boot and driving it in.

"Fuck youuuuuu!" she screamed.

I had to swallow back bile as I watched the shaven headed man lurch backward, two arms pressed against his face, red liquid leaking out between his fingers as he stumbled. What the fuck was I getting myself in to?

No time to find out. With a *thump* I crashed into the remaining man who wasn't holding Yumi. I had launched myself with a jump, using my momentum and his head as a lever. The sudden swiftness of my attack caught him off guard, and putting all my weight to bear I managed to tip him over, landing on his head with the full force of my weight as we crashed into the ground.

"Weren't expecting that, were you, you wanker." I gasped, pleased at my successful assault. The adrenaline was flowing and I felt good, kicking some bad-guy arse. Whoever the fuck they were.

Unfortunately, it seemed the guy's head was made of rock rather than the more common flesh and bone because instead of passing out, or you know, dying, like a normal person would at such a sudden shock to the skull, he instead wrapped his arms around my body, pressing himself tight against me.

Before I knew it he had twisted us onto our sides, locked in the most unsexy embrace I'd ever had the misfortune to be involved in. His dark eyes stared into mine with an intense ferocity and I knew he intended to crush me to death if I didn't stop him first.

"F—" I tried to say but couldn't as my breath began to be squashed right out of me. My arms were locked against my sides as he crushed me, and so instead I frantically tried to injure him with my legs, bringing my right knee up rapidly into the side of his body. I couldn't get much leverage though and it didn't do anything to relax his tight hold.

I looked around wildly and wriggled, desperate to escape as my oxygen began to to run low.

I wasn't going to die like this, damnit. Frantically I tried to knee him again, and this time caught him a good one on the thigh. I heard a slight sound emanate from him, not quite a squeal but a noise of complaint of some kind, certainly.

It wasn't enough. He was on top of me now, squeezing so, so, hard. Shit. Was this it?

Smash. His grip loosened and relaxed completely. I raised my eyebrows and grinned, as I rolled and threw him off of me.

My savior. My bright blond avenging angel. Standing over us, Lucy was looking glorious as she held the remains of the bottle of Maker's Mark Chad and I had been drinking earlier.

I basked in her halo for a moment. Or maybe it was just the fluorescent tube behind her head.

"You're an angel." I told her.

"You're punch drunk," she answered but from the smile on the corners of her lips I knew she'd like the compliment.

"What about the other two?" I asked as I slowly

got up to my feet.

Lucy nodded her head to the side with a grin, and as I stood up again I could see exactly what was going on with the other two gangsters.

Holy shit! Lucy's friend Nicole was pointing a gun at the remaining two men, who still held Yumi between them. There seemed to be some kind of impasse.

Where the fuck had that come from? Call me sheltered, but I'd never actually seen anyone with a real-to-life handgun before, apart from the American cops we'd seen since we arrived. And this little college girl was carrying, and apparently willing to use one! Holy shit.

"Let her go, assholes," said Nicole in a voice that brooked no argument.

They stared at her impassively. What the fuck was wrong with them? If someone pointed a gun at me you know I'd be doing exactly what they said in an instant. *Yes, ma'am. No, ma'am. Three bags full ma'am.*

"You've got to the count of three. One,"

They didn't move. The ballsy fuckers didn't move an inch.

"Two." She shook her head at them in sadness, like she was about to put down a lame horse or something.

"Th—"

The men released Yumi's arms and shouted out some gibberish in their foreign language.

"Thank Christ for that!" I said, apparently more relieved than they were that they hadn't just been blasted to pieces by the steely-eyed college student.

"Shut the hell up," said Nicole and gestured toward the door.

The men gave her baleful glares before the slightly older looking one said some sharp, foreign words to the younger. They released Yumi, but not until they'd barked something at her. After releasing the girl they grabbed their two companions, both of whom were now able to stumble, and headed out the door.

Chad made his way over, brushing imaginary dust off the lapels of his jacket.

"Thanks Chad, you were right, these strip clubs

are great," I said, giving him a hearty piss-taking slap on the shoulder.

He didn't respond. I guess he was still in shock from the attack. Usually you couldn't shut him up, but now he was just kind of standing around in a stunned silence. I should let him bring me to more places like this, I thought.

"What's the matter? Cat got your tongue?"

He didn't seem to hear me, but was watching the departing backs of the four dark suited men. I shrugged my shoulders.

"Come on, let's get out of here." It was Lucy's friend, Nicole, giving the orders.

The gun had disappeared, presumably back into her handbag. I didn't need much persuading. I didn't want to be here if those mafiosos came back with some more of their friends. If it hadn't been for Nicole and her handgun we would've been royally screwed as it was. We could have taken two of them, but four? No way, not without Nicole and her gun. If they came back with more people, or with weapons... I shuddered at the thought.

I wrapped an arm protectively around Lucy's shoulders. She leaned in and damn, did she smell good. Sweet and delicious. I hoped she'd stopped with the rubbish about not coming back with me tonight now. It kind of hurt to breathe and I didn't think I had the energy to be picking her up and carrying her back with me that night.

Johnny

"Come on, let's go," I said.

We were outside the stripclub and it looked calm. There were black tire marks on the surface of the lot next to the door and the air smelt faintly of rubber. Our gangster friends must have left in a hurry.

Hopefully not to get reinforcements.

"I'll get us some Ubers," said Chad.

He meant that new service where you can call cabs just using your smartphone. Except they're not actually cabs, they're like private drivers. Or something. I didn't really understand it to be honest. But getting a car and getting the hell out of here sounded fine to me. Nicole shook her head.

"No, we've got to get away from here first. Let's head over there." Nicole pointed up the highway toward the large neon-lit 24 hour grocery store that was half a mile up the road.

"And just how are we doing to do that without a

car," Chad said with a sigh of exasperation as if he were explaining the problem to a particularly dimwitted child.

"We walk, Chad," I told him.

Nicole nodded.

"Walk? What the hell does that mean?"

I tilted my head at him. What was wrong with him. "Yes, Chad. Walk. You know, one-two, one-two..." I said as I gave him a helpful mime to explain the concept.

"But this is L.A.!"

"If you stay here you might not live."

Another exasperated sigh from Chad. "You know what, that might be preferable."

I laughed. "To walking?"

Nicole apparently didn't have as much time for his nonsense as I did. "Fine. You stay here and wait for your gangster buddies. We're walking over there, then we're going to get us a couple of cars. Okay?"

Nicole started moving, Yumi right beside her. I wrapped an arm around Lucy's shoulders and we started to follow.

"Fine. Fine. I'll walk. But if anyone sees me I'm telling them you kidnapped me."

"So what was the deal with those guys?" I asked Yumi. When you risk your life to save someone you hardly know it's nice to get at least a little bit of an explanation.

She frowned in thought.

"They say I work for them."

"This is about a *job*?" I asked, incredulous.

"They want me work for them. Two year. Three year. Five year. Massage shop. Not good."

"Massage shop, huh?" asked Chad, perking up.

"Yeah. Not good. They say I have to work there, pay off money."

"What money?" I asked. Had she borrowed a ton of money and got herself in debt, I wondered.

"No *real* money. They trick me. They say, 'We give you good job in America, make lots of money. First pay back transport and recruitment charge.'"

Well, that didn't seem too unreasonable. "How much?"

"Ten thousand dollar."

"That's a lot. "

"Yeah. Too much. Too much."

Lucy had been quiet before, but now she piped up. "How's the pay?"

"One customer — they pay one hundred fifty dollar, two hundred dollar.

"Whoah. For a massage? That's pretty good."

"They pay that. But I get just ten dollar. Ten dollar! And not just massage. Special massage."

We were making good progress down the road, it wouldn't take long to get to the parking lot of the store and, hopefully, safety.

"Just ten dollars? What the fuck..."

"Yeah. And I pay room rent fee. Meal fee. Forty dollar per day."

"Oh shit."

"It's not good job."

"Well, that's an understatement," said Nicole.

"That's not a job, that's slavery."

"It's fucked," agreed Nicole.

"Massage huh? With happy endings? How about fifty bucks, I got it right here?" asked Chad.

Nicole dropped back a step and slapped Chad across the face. Hard.

"What the hell!" screeched Chad in shock. He actually sounded injured. "I'm trying to help. That's forty bucks more than she usually gets."

"Chad," I said, "probably be best if you shut up now."

"Only trying to help… some people..."

We carried on trudging down the road. Even though the grass verge was rough and uneven it was still actually rather pleasant. Much better than waiting outside that club for the goons to come back. One step after the other, we continued on mostly in silence.

"Where are you going to go?" I finally asked Yumi.

"I got cousin. San Diego. I try there."

That sounded like a good idea. Get away from here at least.

"You think you'll be okay there?"

She shrugged. "Sure. Why not. Better than here, right?"

"I suppose so."

Finally we reached the edge of the parking lot, but it was surrounded by a drainage ditch and a chain link fence. We had to keep going another hundred yards to the entrance proper before we could get off the road. Finally, we made it.

"Today's a historic day," announced Chad.

We turned to look at him.

"I believe that is the first time I've walked since I moved to this cursed City of Angels when I was an eighteen year old no-nothing country bumpkin."

I laughed.

"It was half a mile, Chad. It's not exactly Hannibal crossing the Alps."

"Half a mile to you, a marathon to me, my friend. And anyway, Hannibal had a big black van."

I shook my head. This guy was unbelievable.

"Now can we *please* get some Ubers?"

I pulled Chad aside a minute. "You want to do something decent?" I asked him a in a low voice.

"What?"

"Pay for Yumi's ride to San Diego. Get her in a car and get her going. I don't want her hanging around

LA."

"A car from here to San Diego? That'd cost..."

"Take it out of our pay, Chad, if you have to, just get it done, okay?"

I was holding him by the shoulder in a collegial embrace, but it was the kind of collegial embrace that could turn into a shoulder-crushing once in a few seconds.

He looked up at me and saw I was serious.

"Okay," he said with a dramatic sigh.

A few minutes later Chad had used three cell phones to book three cars. One for Yumi, one for Nicole and Chad, and one for me and Lucy.

Chad said he needed to talk to Nicole about something. Probably to do with security - it was her biker boyfriend who were doing the security for all of our shows. That meant it was just me and Lucy in our car. When the black Benz finally pulled up I was glad the night was finally over.

Johnny

"What the hell is this? I thought we were going back to the hotel."

Lucy was looking at our new digs, a significant downgrade from the swanky place we'd spent our first night.

"This is the new hotel," I told her. "We got kicked out of the last one, and that's why we are now in this fleapit. They tell me it was very *in* in the 50's. Or maybe it was the 20's. You can thank Chad Chad Price for this fine selection."

She wrinkled her nose in distaste. "You know, I don't think Mr. Price really likes you."

I punched her playfully on the arm. "No, baby. He loves us. Every time something goes wrong he tells us it's all part of his master plan. Don't you trust him?"

"About as far as I could throw him."

"Well he *is* pretty aerodynamic. Did you see the way he flew threw the air earlier after Kim and co.

tossed him?"

She giggled.

I took her inside across the deserted lobby and upstairs in the juddering elevator to our room. Well, it was my room really, but I liked the idea of calling it our room. Though from the way she'd been talking to me earlier I didn't think she would feel the same.

The earlier, urgent lust that I had felt in the club was no longer there. She had, of course, helped to relieve it with the aid of her rather dexterous lower half. And then, there had been the fight. My ribs were rather sore from that experience and I knew I'd be bruised tomorrow. To be honest, what I could really have done with was a good eight hour kip. Not very rock 'n' roll I know, but sometimes a man needs his rest.

We entered the room and the little light at the door came on as we entered. I slipped the plastic rectangle attached to the metal key (no fancy card key here) into its holder and the lights flickered on. I killed most of them with a slap of my hand on the panel.

We made our way across the threadbare carpet which had clearly seen better days — scratch that —

had seen better decades. My hand was on her lower back, guiding her across the room. Her blonde hair seemed to glimmer silver in the low light.

Before I passed out on the bed there was something I needed to do first. I had to get to the bottom of what she'd started to tell me earlier. About how she couldn't see me again. To get at what she meant about me being too dangerous — I *had* been pretty badass earlier, but that was *after* she'd called me dangerous — and about how we couldn't be together. Why did she have to be so serious, I wondered. We'd only just met. I needed to find out what was going on in that pretty little head of hers. Why the hell was she talking about *being together* after one night of, admittedly awesome, sex.

Of course I had reservations of my own too. There were parts of me I wasn't willing to reveal to her yet — hell even to myself if I was honest.

"Earlier, in the…". I paused and stopped myself from saying *strip club*. "Where we were, why did you say you weren't coming back with me tonight?"

We had stopped in front of the king-sized bed

(the best thing about this room) and she turned around to face me.

"Shut up." She smacked me on the chest, hard.

I raised my eyebrows and tilted my head. I open my mouth to begin to ask something, "B—"

Her other hand lifted into the air and went right for my face. My eyes widened. It turned out she wasn't actually slapping me. Instead she was just clapping her hand over my mouth. It seemed she *really* didn't want to talk about whatever it was she *had* wanted to talk about earlier.

The hand that had been on my chest dropped down to the crotch of my jeans. She gave a gentle but firm squeeze and my eyes dropped down, past the perky outline of her breasts, to stare at her pretty little fingers which were fully engaged in groping me.

There's nothing quite like it, is there? Nothing quite like having a horny young girl barely out of her teens desperate for your cock, so desperate in fact she can't keep her hands off. I guess it's something you can never grow tired of. The idea of being wanted, of knowing that you turn them on just by existing, the idea that the girl is getting all hot and wet between her legs at the thought of you putting your cock or tongue or fingers or whatever inside her.

That look in her eyes, that hand on my junk. Suddenly I didn't feel so tired after all. And I didn't yet have my answers. Maybe I could fuck them out of her.

She fondled me gently as she said, "That fight. The men, the guns, you tackling that thug, all of that. You know what it did to me?"

The opposite of what it did to me apparently.

"What?" I asked, my voice raspy with tiredness.

She raised herself up on tiptoes and whispered in my ear, "It makes me very, very," she was rubbing me through the thick fabric of my jeans as she spoke, "*very* horny."

And do you know what makes me horny? A sexy little twenty-something whispering in my ear that she's horny. That'll do it every time.

I wonder if that makes me a weirdo?

I looked down at her as she fumbled with the buttons of my jeans. Her eyes were blazing and I quivered at her rough touch as she got my jeans down as quick as she could.

Were all American girls like this, I wondered. So wild, and forward and uninhibited in telling you exactly what they want? Damn, it was like the jumbo jet that had brought us here had landed in heaven. At least in terms of women. Well, woman. There'd only been her, Lucy.

She yanked down my boxer shorts and grasped my hardness between her tiny, delicate fist, slowly pumping me. It was refreshing having a girl not afraid to let you know what she wants, that was for sure.

She looked up at me, gorgeous cherry painted lips slightly parted, and I was pulled inexorably toward her like metal filings to a magnet. She was completely and absolutely irresistible.

I pressed my lips hungrily against hers and reached behind her, grabbing her ass, which was surprisingly round considering her slight figure. I gave it a hard squeeze and decided, yet again, that it was just about the most touchable, squeezable ass I'd ever encountered.

She whimpered as our tongues found each other,

hot and thrusting and writhing, unable to get enough. Our lips parted for a second, then met, then parted then met again in a flurry of quick kisses.

"I fuckin' love how horny you get," I told her.

"I love how horny you make me," she said looking up at me with determination in her eyes.

She grabbed me by the hair and walked two steps backward before falling onto the bed, pulling me down with her.

Lucy didn't pull my head to meet hers, and nor did she pull it lower to meet her delightfully perky little breasts.

This was a girl who knew exactly what she wanted, and right now what she wanted was my mouth and tongue between her legs and she wasn't afraid to let me know.

"Eat me, you English asshole. Eat me," she said with a moan.

You don't have to ask me twice. With her help we quickly had her completely naked on the surprisingly crisp, white sheets.

"Hurry up," she said, writhing on the bed, her

hands roaming over her own body, over her tits, and thighs and her wet slit.

I couldn't help but take a moment to admire her in her naked glory. She was beautiful. *Beautiful.* As beautiful as any girl I'd ever seen. But I only stared for a moment, after all, she didn't seem to the patient type.

I grasped her by the thighs and found myself shivering as I lowered my mouth to her smooth and ever so wet lips.

My own set of damp lips met her slick softness and I let my tongue slip out in an inquisitory taste.

"Fuck!"

I jerked my head up.

She grabbed my hair and mashed my head back down between her silky thighs, back to the taste of heaven.

"That was a ..." she panted, "good..." she moaned as my tongue reached her again, "'fuck'".

I ran my hands up her calves, her thighs, around the sides of her ass and hips, over her belly and up to the perfect little mounds above.

I used my lips and my tongue to first taste, and

probe, and tease. As my hand reached her breasts I began to circle around her clit with my tongue eliciting moans and whimpers and squeals.

My fingers pressed against her nipples, then squeezed. She grabbed one of my hands with hers and pushed my fingers. She wanted me to squeeze harder. Who am I to deny a lady a little pain with her pleasure?

With a firm press of my fingers I began to oblige, squeezing hard, releasing and squeezing hard again as I worked my tongue and mouth giving her kisses and caresses.

She let out a loud moan and then with a suddenness that caused my head to be crushed against her pelvis she wrapped her thighs around my neck pulling me into her so deep I thought I'd suffocate. What a glorious way to go that would be. *British Rocker Found Dead in Seedy LA Hotel - Cause: Cunnilingus*. That'd be sure to make me famous.

Hot, and wet and delicious I licked, and teased her until it was time to take her all the way. I knew it was time because my tongue was getting sore (not that I would ever tell her that.)

I worked on her clit in a constant rhythm with my tongue. Whereas before I'd been teasing her with a range of flicks, and kisses, prods and licks, now I was using one smooth, constant motion to bring her to the edge.

She panted, faster and faster. The vice around my head got tighter and tighter. I squeezed and released and squeezed and released her nipples harder and harder.

"Fuck you," she gasped and I felt her body quiver. Her thighs gave me another squeeze like she was trying to take my head off, and I could feel her lower body quivering and shaking like there was an earthquake going on. My tongue sensed her fluttering and I took her between my lips. I squeezed her nipples hard and she squealed again.

While she was seeing stars I think I was too. Finally she released my head, letting her thighs fall back down, legs open again. My hands just held her breasts now, and I raised my head, surprised at how cool the air was outside of her delicious honey trap.

"Holy fuck," she whispered.

I grinned in self-satisfaction as I slid up the bed and lay on my back next to her, also panting as I finally tasted cool air again.

"I'm pretty good at that, aren't I?"

She let out a soft giggle, and poked at my arm.

"You think so, huh?"

"Oh yeah. You were shaking and moaning and quivering—"

"Quivering huh?"

"Yep. You were *totally* quivering, and I thought you were just about to crush my head."

"Nah, I was just crushing your head because you're so annoying. I was worried you might try to start talking."

Lying little minx. I knew she had just been terrified I'd dare tease her by taking my mouth off of her again.

My left arm was drifting up and down her soft body. Over the mounds of her perky breasts, and down between the damp cleft between her legs. It was the kind of body you just couldn't get enough of. I wanted — no, *needed* — to touch every bit of it, taste every last inch of it, squeeze and hug her and never let her go.

Damn, I thought, there must be something in the water around here. What was wrong with me thinking like this. Oh well, it was nice while it was lasting. It was nice to have someone to want, someone who wanted *you*, someone you just couldn't get enough of. In fact, in some ways she was almost enough. Almost enough to make me forget about those other desires that sometimes came over me, but which I had successfully avoided all these years.

I let the middle finger of my hand slip between her legs, sliding easily and deeply inside her and eliciting another soft moan. I pulled it out and raised it to my lips for another sweet taste of her. My other hand was wrapped around my cock and I was slowly, lazily jerking myself off while I still recovered my breath.

Before we'd entered the room I'd been intent on talking to her and passing out. After what had just happened though I had something else more pressing on my mind. Or in my hand, anyway.

When I felt I was about to explode because I couldn't take it anymore I rolled on top of her pressing my hard chest against her breasts and resting my weight on my forearms. I stared down into her eyes which I knew to be ridiculously blue in the daytime, but were now only vaguely gray in the dim light of this room. My body was above hers, my legs were between hers, and I was just about fit to explode.

It's a powerful feeling isn't it? When you're lying above a beautiful girl who's smaller, lighter and weaker than you (and I'm not sure I'd want to meet one who's bigger, heavier and stronger than me). Just the knowledge that they are yours for the taking, that you can do anything you want to them and they're perfectly willing to take it.

And now I was going to take her.

Lucy

My body was still giving tiny little flutters and contractions as I lay back basking in the afterglow of a seriously intense orgasm. He really knew what he was doing with his tongue. At first I'd thought I was going to have to give him some guidance, but he'd just been teasing, building me up before he really got to work. Hot damn that was intense.

I glanced to my side, he was panting softly and was using one hand to pump himself while he ran the other over my body. I guessed I really turned him on. I just have that effect on people, y'know?

One of the benefits of getting a guy really turned on, really all hot and bothered is that it encourages them to really go for it. When they just can't take it anymore because they're so hot for you they can really give it to you — hard.

His hand left my body and he used the arm to prop himself up beside me, then he rolled on top of me, so hot and big and hard and strong above me. I felt an involuntary flutter again, like an aftershock after a large earthquake as he hung above me.

"My turn."

A tiny whimper escaped from between my pursed lips and my heart began to beat faster, pounding my ribcage.

There's something about a slightly older guy, someone who's been around a bit and knows what he's doing with a girl's body that really helps. I didn't get those girls back at the college who just wanted to date the other college boys. I mean sure, some of them looked good, but could they *really* look after a girl, a *woman*? Nuh-uh. All brag and no performance. A girl like me needs to be treated *right* and I just can't get that from some little college boy.

Now this guy, this foreign British guy hanging above me, hard cock resting against my belly, staring lustfully into my eyes. This was someone who could do a girl right.

I was lying back, under him, completely at the mercy of him. He could do whatever he wanted to me right now and I was almost shivering at the thought of it.

"Your turn?" I whispered.

He leaned in for another one of those glorious kisses. Tasting faintly of bourbon and mint gum, but mostly of me, his hot lips pressed against mine sending electricity surging through my body. It only lasted a few seconds and when he parted our lips I tried to grab him to pull him back down to me but to no avail. He was too strong.

"My turn."

He kneeled up above me looking glorious.

He was gorgeous. His body told a story, through half a dozen sizable tattoos. His time on the stage, strutting about and whatever else singers did had given him washboard abs that demanded a hand be run across them. His hair hung down, framing his face and it was all I could do to stop myself moaning at how stupidly hot he looked, kneeling over me like a tiger trying to decide just how it was going to deal with its captured prey.

I reached out, wanting to touch his hard cock

again, to squeeze it in my hands, to pump it and taste it, to let him fuck my mouth.

I wanted to please him like he'd pleased me.

As I reached out he he didn't let my hand reach him though. Instead he grabbed me by the wrist, and the other hand grabbed my thigh.

With a quick movement of his arms he flipped me over and my head flumped into the pillow below me.

A surge of excitement ran through me. Whereas a moment before I had wanted to pleasure him with my mouth and hands, I knew now that what he wanted was something different. And he was going to do just whatever it was that he wanted.

I love it when a man takes control. When he knows what he wants and he just takes it. *That* was something no college boy had ever done. When you're all hot and bothered and willing and lying under them but they keep being overly polite instead of giving you the good hard-fucking you need it takes something away. Where's the animal passion? Where's the virility? *Excuse me, but do you mind if I touch you there? Is it okay if I do this? Is it alright if I put my hand here?* Fuck that.

Turning my head to the side I asked, "What do you want?"

"You," he said in a breathless voice.

He grabbed me near the hips and lifted my ass into the air.

"Fuck me," I whimpered, "fuck me however you want."

"I will."

I was hot and wet and ready for him. While before I thought his eating me out would be the main attraction, now I knew that was just a taster.

He was kneeling behind me and with two strong hands he pulled my thighs open. I raised myself up onto all fours.

Doggy, huh?

"Stay down."

With a sweep of his hands he pulled my arms away from me and my head dropped back down to the pillow.

Not doggy, then. Just head down and —

"Ohh—" I said, muffled into the pillow.

With urgent swiftness he had grabbed me by the hair while at the same time placing the head of his cock inside me.

No more foreplay.

He was ready to fuck and that's exactly what he was going to do.

With a yank my rocker pulled my hair back with one hand, squeezed a nipple hard with the other and—

"Fuuuu —"

—thrust deep inside me, filling me up completely with his thick, hard cock.

I was under him, controlled by him and filled by him. What more could a horny girl ask for?

"You like that." It wasn't a question. It was a statement that brooked no argument.

I could just about speak with his hair pulling my mouth away from the pillow now.

"Mmm. I ... like ... that ..." I said between pants.

He shoved himself into my savagely, holding me in place with his breast-squeezing hand and his firm grip on my hair.

"You like being fucked from behind?"

I squealed. "I like... being fucked... however..."

Harder and more frantic thrusts.

"However?" There was a hint of annoyance in his voice and his next few thrusts were harder and stronger.

I was already gasping for breaths as he worked his magic inside me, filling me up so deeply and with such force I could barely remember my own name, let alone make coherent sentences.

"However... you... want..." I managed to get out.

"However I want, huh?"

Faster and more urgently he pushed into me, his groin slapping hard against my ass and bouncing off again with each thrust.

He gave a tug of my hair and a rough squeeze of my nipples that hurt *so* good.

"Use me... anything..."

He was going faster and faster now, fucking me hard and rough. After the day we'd had it was the perfect antidote, the perfect way to recover. Everything faded away, all the events and worries of the last few days. Tuition fees, stripping jobs, violent thugs, downgraded hotels — it all disappeared.

"Anything huh? How about I fuck you... until I'm ready... then I cum... in your mouth..." he panted, "in your mouth... and all over... that pretty little face?"

Whatever he wanted, I wanted.

"Cum on my face, my ... mouth... my... lips," I told him.

His hand released from groping my breasts and then...

SMACK. He slapped my ass hard, and it stung like a bitch sending a red hot glow through my body.

"You're a dirty little girl, aren't you?"

The sharp sting faded and the throbbing pain became just a glorious addition to everything else he was doing to my body. The busy hand that wasn't grabbing my hair moved back to my breast and gave another hard squeeze.

I let out a whimper. I was close to the edge again.

"Only... for you."

Another rough squeeze, followed by a twist on my hard nipple which made me gasp. Then... *SMACK*, again, he slapped my ass.

"You're *my* dirty little girl?"

I whimpered assent and as he did so he pounded into me harder than ever.

"Ahhh—"

That was it. He'd done it again. My ears roared with the sound of silence as my lower body quaked and shook and I felt the electric warmth spread through my entire body.

"Did I make my dirty little girl cum again?"

I could do nothing, say nothing, just let out a groan. If he hadn't been holding me up by my hair I would have collapsed back down onto the bed.

SMACK. Another glorious hit to my ass and a pounding thrust of his hot and hard cock sent the heat rolling back through me. Would this never end?

"Answer me."

"Uhh... yeahhhhh," I finally managed to get out.

"Yes what?"

"You... made me... cum… again," I said panting between each gasped out word.

His pace behind me was frantic now as he neared his climax. With one slap after another he pounded into me sending hot jolt after hot jolt through my confused, shaking body.

Then, he pushed my head back down into the pillow, forcing my body away from him as he withdrew.

A moment of aching emptiness. My moan of disappointment muffled by the pillow below.

But only a moment. When he was out of me he released his grip on my hair and using two hands around my hips roughly flipped me over. He pulled me to a low kneeling position and grabbed me by the hair again. He kneeled higher on his legs, his massive engorged cock, wet with my juices, just in front of my face.

Holding the back of my head with one hand, he used the other to hold himself.

I knew what he wanted and I wanted to give it to him. I parted my lips and he thrust the head of his cock inside, so hot and hard yet silky smooth on the outside. I wrapped my lips around him and as he did so he placed the other hand behind my head. He held me tight like a vice and thrust his hips urgently into my mouth to finish himself off.

"Fuuuu—"

I couldn't move my head, all I could do was use my tongue on his cock and look up at him, wide eyed.

He gazed into my eyes for a moment and then his head dropped back, he thrust himself deep into my mouth let out a guttural moan that was half swear word and half primal growl as he finished.

Johnny

I was awoken in the best possible way. God knows what hour in the morning it was when Chad grabbed my shoulder, gave it a squeeze, shook it, and an annoyingly chirpy voice said, "Rise and shine, Champ." The shaking continued. "Come on buddy, get up."

Oh wait, scratch that, it was actually the worst way to wake up in the world.

I blinked my eyes open lazily several times. I looked up to see the besuited little man who was currently acting as my band manager. To make matters worse, when I reached to the side to grab Lucy's tits or a piece of ass to cheer me up there was no one there. She'd gone. Again.

It was only just beginning but already today was shaping up to be a terrible day. Light was streaming through the closed curtains; they were so thin and threadbare they didn't act as much of a barrier to the morning rays streaming in. How long had I slept, I wondered. It couldn't have been more than a couple of hours, and in fact it felt like I'd only just closed my eyes. *I'm never drinking again. I'm never going to a stripclub again. I'm never—*

"Come on, I've got half a dozen bassists waiting for you to audition them."

My hands clutched the side of my head. That was right. My goddamned bassist had gone missing. And now we had to find a temporary replacement until Chad's top investigation team had managed to track him down.

"What do you mean they're waiting? They're at the studio already?"

"Studio? What studio?"

"Well, where are we doing the auditions. Did you have somewhere else in mind?"

Chad was pacing up and down the room. "We're doing the auditions downstairs, in Conference Room C."

How the hell was he so cheery? He can't have slept much more than I did but he was all bright-eyed and bushy tailed. Annoying twat.

"So we're auditioning them in a meeting room are we? That's great, Chad. Really great."

"I figured all you need to do is see whether they can play on not. Surely the acoustics or whatever don't matter, do they?"

"For a man involved in the music industry, you seem to know remarkably little about it."

"Baby, you do the music stuff, I do the business stuff. I'm going to make you, me, and the rest of the band both rich, and famous."

I closed my eyes to get a couple more minutes rest. I wasn't sure I had the energy to do with much attention.

"By the way, what'd you do with the stripper?"

I blinked my eyes open again. "She's *not* a stripper."

"Yeah, and I'm not the best damn manager in the industry."

I felt a burst of annoyance. This guy. At this time of the morning. Urgh.

"I don't know, Chad."

"Should have slipped her another fifty-spot to stay the night."

Using my hands I pushed myself to a sitting position, leaning back against the headboard. I grabbed the glass of water that was next to the bed — when had I put that there, I wondered. Or maybe she did it. I took a gulp.

"I'd appreciate it if you stopped calling my girl—" Oops, what did I nearly say? "My friend a stripper, or implying she's a prostitute."

"Me too, asshole," came a voice from the bathroom as the door swung open and a towel clad blonde-haired angel emerged.

She hadn't left. I suddenly felt a whole lot less hung over and the day seemed much more promising.

"Tell them I'll be down in fifteen," I said to Chad who was staring at Lucy with an appraising look and nodding to himself, "and put your tongue back in your mouth."

"Make it ten. We've got a whole bunch of bassists to get through, then you've got to do an interview, then there's a security meeting, you've got another lunchtime interview, and then we've got to get to the venue."

So. Much. To. Do.

"He'll be down in a minute, Chad," she said, walking back toward the bed, "he's got something else to do first."

I was liking this girl more and more.

"Bye, Chad," I said. He was half out the door.

Delighted, I saw the anguish on his face as the door closed just as Lucy dropped her fluffy white towel to the floor.

Something else to do first, indeed.

Lucy

We were backstage after the show in the club's crappy little excuse for a green room and he looked exhausted. Wide eyed, elated, but exhausted. That didn't mean he was going to get a night off though. Nuh uh.

A girl's got needs, you know. And right now I had a very particular need, a very particular craving. I sidled up to him, squeezing his upper arm and feeling the contours of the biceps underneath.

"You know what I want?"

He looked at me cautiously. "What?"

I giggled and fluttered my eyelashes at him. "Guess."

He looked around warily but everyone else was just talking or wandering off. No one was listening.

"You want to suck me off again, right?" he said in a quiet voice.

I punched him on the arm.

"Can't you think about something else for once?"

He raised his arms defensively, his eyes wide.

"I thought *you* couldn't think of anything else. "

"Well, that may be true some of the time."

"A *lot* of the time," he rejoined.

"Quite a lot of the time. But not *all* the time."

"Sometimes what a girl wants is..." I paused to tease him some more.

He looked at me even warily now.

"Some good, no, make that *great*..."

I stood up on tiptoes and whispered in his ear, "Italian."

He tilted his head to the side and let out a soft sigh.

"I'm English, I'm afraid..."

Was he teasing me? Acting dumb? Or acting like *I'm* dumb.?

"Italian *food*."

"Ahhh. Pizza?"

I shook my head. I'd found this great place online earlier. I'd got distracted after I'd made the mistake of googling *Easy ways for a hot college girl to make lots of money* and come up short on anything that wasn't a scam or some kind of prostitution. Then one click had led to another and... I was browsing Yelp listings for nearby restaurants.

And nearby happened to be one that was open until way late at night. Apparently it caters to a real European crowd. According to one of the reviews I'd read in their culture *it's not uncommon for people to go for dinner at 10 p.m. and still be eating at midnight.*

"So, what? Spag bol?"

I frowned at him. "No. Some real, authentic stuff. I'm talking *caponata, Spaghetti al ricci, Cannoli...* the people who run it are straight off the boat from Sicily."

"I don't know what any of that stuff is, but I think they come by plane now. " He said, teasing me.

I fake kicked him and he fake acted like it hurt.

"Ow," he said, wincing. "Isn't it a bit late? It's like... nearly eleven. It's gonna' be shut, surely?"

"I told   you, it's genuine European style. Don't you Euros all eat dinner at like, eleven o'clock or something?"

He frowned. "I'm *not* European, I'm English. Or

British. But *not* European..."

Oh good. Another chance to tease.

"That's not what the map says. The map says England's in Europe."

"Well the map's stupid. Anyway, no, we don't normally eat dinner this late where *I'm* from. My Mum always gave us our tea at 6:30 sharp," he said before conceding, "but I am pretty peckish."

"Good," I said and with perfect timing my phone buzzed, "the car's here."

He laughed. "Already? How'd you know I'd say yes."

I shrugged. "If you didn't I'd go on my own."

"You would, huh?"

"Yep. Or maybe I'd ask the driver to join me."

He laughed. "You little slut," he said and poked my arm.

I giggled and whispered up into his ear. "But I'm only your little slut." As I walked off I turned and said over my shoulder, "For the moment."

"For the moment?"

"Come on."

I didn't need to be getting to that, having *that* conversation right now. How was I going to explain it to him? *Why* was I going to explain it to him? This music tour of his was only going to last a week anyway, why not just have fun for a week then let him jet off back to Europe. I mean England.

But I knew I couldn't. He was doing something to me. Making me feel things I didn't *want* to be feeling. Not because of a problem with him per se, but because he was going to be leaving soon.

But then... but then... maybe... nah.

I'm not a romantic. Usually. I'm *practical*. I may be wild, but I'm also down to earth. I'm no 'pie in the sky', 'everything's going to be alright', 'love will find away' wide-eyed idealist. No way.

Unless...

"Come on, I thought you said the car was here." He was holding me by the elbow.

I shook my head to clear it and we headed out of the venue.

Still, that was something to look forward to now. *Sortinos*. Some real Sicilian food.

I let a smile cross my lips as I let myself indulge in more ridiculous daydreams as he guided me to the car with a hand on my lower back.

* * *

The place was small but had a warm, cozy atmosphere. There were maybe a dozen tables, each one covered with a simple white table cloth. There were two dark haired, Italian-looking waiters in black shirts with perhaps one button too many undone at the top, and one dyed-blond waitress who was acting as a greeter.

"Table for two?"

I nodded. "Yes please."

"Do you have a reservation?"

I nodded. "Yep. Name of Wild. Lucy Wild."

She frowned as she looked at the printout in front of her. Johnny too was giving me a strange look.

"Umm I only just made the booking, like, an hour ago. Maybe it's not on your list yet."

She frowned and continued to peer at the paper as if a new name might spontaneously appear. Johnny tapped me on the shoulder.

"You're name's not *Wild*," he said.

I shrugged. "It's my alternative persona."

"Your what?"

I grinned. "You know, like... a stage name, or a pen name. And right now I'm on vacation, and Lucy Wild is out to play."

He shook his head in bemusement.

The greeter tapped the paper and looked up at us again. "No name here. But we've got a table free anyway. I've gotta get Dad to put a screen out here. But he says paper was good enough for *his* Papa and for Nonno," she let out a sigh and brushed her hair out of her eyes. "Come on."

I grinned up at Johnny as the girl turned on her low black heels to lead the way.

"Nice huh?"

"Pretty swish, pretty swish indeed."

I let him take my arm and lead me behind the waitress. Johnny was wearing a suit jacket over a white t-shirt and his regular dark blue jeans. He looked good, and with the last minute addition of the jacket looked just about formal enough for *Sortino's*. Not that it was a classy joint as such, but most of the customers had at least made a bit of an effort. If Johnny had still been wearing the black sweaty t-shirt he'd had on on the stage we would have felt out of place.

He ran his hair hand through his hair. I wondered if he knew how sexy he looked doing that. It was a habit of his, and the female half of his audience swooned every time he did it.

We were taken over to a table in a kind of alcove in a corner of the restaurant. There were low walls topped with potted plants surrounding two sides, with one side open and another side being the full restaurant wall.

In the center of the table was an old wine bottle in which was replaced a single white flower. Simple but elegant in a homely kind of way.

As we reached the table Johnny stepped forward and pulled out a straight-backed wooden chair and nodded his head toward me. I grinned with a flutter in my stomach. Sometimes it's just the little things, you know?

We sat down and were given glasses of water and

a leather-bound menu book each.

"How was the new bassist?" I asked him.

"Do you mind if I get technical with you?" he asked me

"Umm. I can't promise to understand it, but sure, go ahead." It's kind of hot when guys are really into their 'thing' whatever their thing is. I just hoped I could at least pretend to understand when he got down to the nuts and bolts. Still, he had warned me.

"Well, in technical, real pro-musician terms..."

"Yes," I said, nodding, and getting ready to pretend to understand.

"Well, his playing was, what we call in the industry..." he said, pausing for effect. He looked at me directly with arched eyebrows. "...bollocks"

I coughed and laughed at the same time in surprise before managing to say, "Wow those technical terms are tough for a layman like me."

He nodded. "Yeah, I know. But sometimes it's the only way, right?"

I rested a hand on his forearm. "You're a goof."

"A 'goof' huh. Can't say I've ever been called

that before." He tapped the menu with a finger. "What are you going to go for?"

"Maybe the calamares, then... hmmm... some kind of pasta. This seafood one looks good.," I said indicating something I didn't think I could quite pronounce.

He raised his eyes at me. "It's got *octopus* in it," he said.

I shrugged. "Yeah, cool, huh?"

He shook his head at me sternly. "No. Not cool. Make sure you keep those sea monsters away from my plate."

"Here. I'll try this one," he said tapping his finger at something on the menu. "This looks a bit more *norma*l."

He spoke with a strange emphasis on the last word that made me not quite trust him. I looked at where he was pointing and then gave him a slap on his sturdy forearm. "Ha. Ha." I said, merely saying the syllables, not actually laughing. The dish he'd chosen was Pasta alla Norma. *Normal* indeed.

"And to start?"

He tapped his chin thoughtfully. "This doesn't look too strange." He jabbed a finger next to the listing that read *gatto di patate - A Traditional Sicilian antipasti consisting of a potato and cheese pie.*

I nodded in approval. Very traditional. I'd quite like to try it myself.

As I closed my menu book and looked up a waiter with melted-chocolate eyes appeared as if by magic. It looked like the service was going to be pretty good here too. He gave us a friendly smile and took our order. We decided to get a bottle of red too. While we wouldn't be doing any *real* drinking, you can't have an Italian meal without a glass of vino, can you?

"Is that everything?"

We told him it was, and as he turned to walk away the girl who'd greeted us at the door appeared with a jug of water, a basket of fresh baked bread and a little bowl of fresh olive oil that smelled almost as good as the Italian bread it was to accompany.

"Let me know if you need any more."

"So what are you going to do about the bassist?"

He let out a sigh and gave a shrug, a look of worry on his brow. "What can I do? I want my real bassist back. Chad has got Lonnie looking for Si. But if he doesn't find him..."

Lonnie was a member of the Sons of Mayhem bikers and was managing security for the The Full Force's shows as they did their one week mini-tour around Southern California. He was also an old friend of Johnny and the rest of the band from when he lived in the UK.

"Then what?"

He shrugged. "You know who I want, if I can't get Si?"

"Who?" I asked.

"Lonnie."

"Lonnie? *Our* Lonnie?" I asked, confused. As far as I knew he was just a biker-cum-security-guy.

He laughed.

"Yeah. *Your* Lonnie. He used to be *our* Lonnie. Not that we call him that back then. And he was a damn-fine bass player."

Huh, how about that. I tapped my chin

thoughtfully, and took another bite of bread.

"Right. I knew you guys knew him back home. But..."

"He didn't tell you he was a musician?" he asked, the corners of his mouth turned up in amusement. "That he used to be in the band?"

I shook my head thoughtfully. "Nope."

He shrugged. "He quit years ago. Said he'd never play again. I promised back then I'd never ask him again. It was never an issue with him being over here, and with Si being in the band. But now, with Si missing and Chad only giving me a bunch of muppets to choose from..."

"Now you want to ask Lonnie, right?"

He shrugged. "This tour is important. Although we're not playing big venues Chad says we're creating a lot of buzz. Oh and he says he has some big secret event planned which he guarantees will get us some major coverage. Sneaky little bastard won't tell me what though."

"A big thing, huh?"

"Yeah. Some secret bullshit. I dunno. He's

promised he's going to make us as big as the Rolling Stones. I'd settle for for as big as Razorlight."

"Who?"

He took a big gulp of wine and said, "Nevermind."

I leaned in. "You'll always be *big* to me."

He gave a little chuckle and said in a low voice, "*You* make me bigger than I've ever been before."

We're terrible, right?

The appetizers were brought over by our friendly waiter who placed them down in front of us. He didn't need to check which of us had ordered what and presented the two plates with beaming smiles.

I took one bite of a crispy-coated calamari.

"Oh. My. God." I wiped my lips with a napkin as I spoke.

He looked at me with alarm.

"What's the matter?"

I gigged. "No. I mean, this is *fantastic* You've got try it."

He wrinkled his nose. "Nah. I don't do that weird

sea stuff."

I frowned at him. "What about fish and chips?"

"That's different, that's *normal* food."

With a sigh I shook my head. I cut another piece in half and dipped it into the garlic mayonnaise sauce. I leaned over toward him, a stern look in my eyes. "I said," waving the fork kind of threateningly, "try it."

He gave a fake gulp. "Umm, since I don't want to get stabbed..." and with a smile he leaned forward and snatched it off the end of my fork."

He grimaced for a second then gave a bite. Then another. His eyes lit up and before I could stop him he was jabbing his fork over at my plate, snagging the other half of the calamari and dipping it back into the sauce.

"Not so terrible, huh?"

He gave me a beaming smile. "Wow. You were right. It's like a mini-chewier fish. And no chips."

"That's a pretty lame description you know."

"Well, it *is*.."

I pulled my plate closer toward me to guard the remaining couple I had left. The portions weren't very big here, though this was just an appetizer.

"How's the pie?"

He looked down at the beautiful circle of crumbly looking pastry and it's yellowish egg top. He looked at me. He looked down again. "It's okay."

I tilted my head to the side. I knew his little game. I reached over with my fork and broke off a good sized piece, probably about a quarter of the small dish.

He grimaced as I attacked his food but didn't open his mouth to complain.

When I got it into my mouth I could see what he'd been doing. He hadn't wanted to share it because it was *that* good. I was impressed he hadn't physically stopped me from taking it. I would have slapped his hand away in an instant. It was spectacular!

"This place is good, huh?"

"You know, I don't usually like fancy places. But this is really... good. And not too posh either. I don't think they're judging us here."

"Yep. We've got to come here again." I said but as I did so a pang of melancholy dropped to my stomach. How long did we have until his tour was over and he'd be heading off back home? And I'd be heading back to try and scrounge up a few bucks before next semester started.

A low chuckle. "Well let's finish *this* time first. Maybe the mains will be horrible." He looked around furtively. "Or maybe you'll get in a fight with the owner."

I squeezed his forearm. "Yeah, right."

Lucy

"So, are you over that crap now?"

I frowned at him.

"What do you mean?"

"You know what I mean." The way you ran off after that first night, and how you were trying to avoid me.

"Until you caught me pretending to be a stripper?"

He chuckled. "Yeah."

"Alright." I'd brought this on myself. I'd have to do this. "There's three problems."

"Shit. Three problems with me already? This is only the third day we've known each other."

I grinned. "Not with you. Not really."

Go on then. Hit me with them. Let me guess. My— " He looked around and said in a low voice, "Y'know," he sat up straight again, "is too much for you to handle, right?"

I giggled. No. That's not it. Your... y'know... is just about perfect."

"Whew" he joked.

I shifted uncomfortably in my seat. "Do we really have to do this?"

He nodded as he used a piece of bread to mop up some of the sauce remaining on his plate.

"Alright. First, you're leaving in, what, a week?"

He nodded.

"Which ties into the second problem, which is that I think... I really think I like you. Like, really like you. Like, a lot."

He grinned. "Really like me, huh? Sounds like a terrible problem."

"Yeah. So that's why I disappeared after that first night. That awesome, awesome, first night. I didn't want to get too drawn in to your... charms..."

He sighed. "Yeah, well. Me too. I really liked you. But that's why I was annoyed. if you really like someone, why try and run?"

"Because you're leaving!"

He nodded. "Well, yeah. But the world's a small

place these days. "

"What does *that* mean. You can't exactly drive from Farmington to London." for an evening.

"Well, no, I guess not. But y'know, the world's full of possibilities now. And you've nearly graduated, right?"

I nodded.

"So who knows. Maybe you'd get a job in the UK. Maybe my band would relocate here. "

"We've known each other three days, Johnny."

He shrugged. "Call me a romantic, but I figure either we're right for each other, in which case things will work themselves out. Or we're just having fun with each other, in which case, let's just have fun, y'know?"

I sighed. It kind of made sense. Kind of.

"I guess I was worried I would fall for *you* and you'd just abandon me. I've never been the kind of girl who mopes and pines after someone and I didn't want to become that girl because of *you.*"

"Well. I face the same risk. Can't we just have fun for a few days and see how we feel?"

He squeezed my hand. I put another hand onto

the table and he grabbed that too. They were so much bigger and stronger than my own.

God, we must have looked sickening sitting at the table, both hands holding each others, staring into each other's eyes... if I'd been at another table looking across at us I'd have been rolling my eyes.

"And the other problem?"

"I'd rather not… just forget it," I told him. I didn't want to get into that now. "I don't, I can't..."

"You can't what, Lucy?"

"I don't think I'm comfortable saying it. I'm sorry. Just forget it."

"What do you mean 'forget it'?" he asked.

"Maybe I'm not sure. Maybe I shouldn't be saying stuff like this unless I'm really sure, y'know?"

"'Y'know'? Are you kidding me?", he put his wine glass down with a hard tap on the table, anger barely controlled. "It's hard for me to understand."

Shit. I was doing poorly.

"Sorry. It's me. It's my fault, I just —"

"Oh shit, one of these it's not you, it's me things? I thought we'd just agreed we'd have fun for a week or two.. and then, maybe..."

"Shut up for a minute," I said. "I'll tell you."

His eyes widened and his lips parted for a moment but then they did, indeed, shut up. I guess he realized I did have something to say and I wanted him to listen.

"Alright. No more talking around the bush. Here it is: I. Am. Fucked. Up." I paused to take a breath.

"N—" he started to say.

I burned him with my laser eyes. Or, well, you know the best I could despite not being a superhero. It worked. He shut up again.

"Just listen, okay? Here it is. I'm laying it out:" I took a sip from my water glass instead of the wine glass for once. I was going to do it. I was going to tell him.

"I can't..." How best to put this? "I mean, I like *you*, and I've liked other guys but I have this.... thing. I just..." Sometimes saying the simplest of things was, in fact, the hardest thing. "I just can't imagine being with *a* man."

He just about spat out his drink and ended up coughing and spluttering.

"What do you mean not being with a man? You sure didn't seem like a lesbian last night."

"You're not listening properly," I said to him, "I can't see myself just being with *a* man. Singular."

"You mean…"

I nodded

"Like I said. I'm fucked up, okay? I just can't imagine being in any kind of real relationship without two men."

"Without *two* men? What two men? I don't even..."

"I mean, like, two lovers..."

"Like a guy in LA and a guy in London?"

I suppressed a giggle. This was serious. I'd never laid it out on the line before like this. What I really felt. What I really was. What a fucked up person I was when it all came down to it.

"No. No. No. I mean, two guys, together. Not like two relationships at once. One relationship. Three people. Like..."

"Like, a threesome?"

I almost giggled. Almost. I think my lips turned

up and my eyes almost sparkled. The look on his face was curious too. I thought he'd be more shocked than he was.

"No, not like a threesome. I mean like..."

"Like?"

"Like a relationship. Umm… like a couple. But with another."

"A couple, but like with another? So, a threesome then?"

"I sighed. " No, a threesome is like some super-awesome kinky one night stand type of thing where you get double penetrated by two super-hot guys, wha—"

Johnny interrupted, "Or two girls. A threesome can definitely be two girls and one guy..."

"Yeah, whatever. But what I'm talking about, is that my fantasy — no, not fantasy, my desire, my need, my future, if I'm to be happy involves me and two guys."

I looked at him suddenly feeling an aching emptiness. I must have ruined it all now, I thought. Why couldn't I just have enjoyed the next few days without messing it all up first. Why did I have to say that.

Maybe we could have been happy without that. Maybe some weird fucked up shit would have happened which would have allowed me to move to England or wherever, or him to move here, and now I'd just fucked it all up by spouting this nonsense. It was nonsense, right? My dreams were surely just that — dreams and nothing more.

As I looked into his eyes, almost hoping for forgiveness, his gaze met mine.

"You know what?" he asked.

"What?" I asked softly.

"That's really, *really* hot."

Jamie

What a meal. She'd told me it'd cheer me up and she'd been right. We were in a little Italian restaurant — *Sicilian* she'd insisted — and it had been just what I needed.

At first I'd been depressed, all moping and complaining (you know, the usual), but then the wine had kicked in... and the food!

Now I felt alive again. The past couple of days I'd been in a kind of daze. A dark cloud hanging over me, my head full of cotton wool, not knowing exactly who I was or what I wanted to be. Would I ever become an actor or a model like I wanted? A *real* one, who actually earned money at it? Would I ever fall in love? Would I ever feel a kick in my step again?

Maybe it was just getting out of the apartment that did it. Maybe that was all I'd needed. But whether it was just getting outside, or some magic with the food and wine, or maybe a combination of it all, I was feeling alive again. Exuberant even. The world was ripe with possibilities and strength was flowing through my veins. Well, strength and alcohol that is.

"You know what, Donna?" I said as I took another sip, that was actually more of a gulp, from my glass.

She tilted her head and gave me a curious look.

"What?"

"I've had it. I've just had it with everything. With everyone." I took another sip. "No more Mr. Niceguy."

She looked at me with a twinkle in her eye and let out what seemed to be an amused chuckle. Couldn't she see I was serious?

"You'll always be a Mr. Niceguy. You haven't got a mean bone in your body."

I couldn't help but let my own lips drift upward in a smile. She was such a darling to me, and maybe she was partly right. But I'm sure I had a mean bone *somewhere*. Everyone does, right? Of course, if I didn't, I could certainly *take* a mean bone...

"I mean, no more hiding. No more pretending I am what I'm not." I thumped my fist down toward the table but caught it just before the impact. Nothing fell over, the cutlery didn't rattle, and the only visible signal was the surfaces of our water and wine glasses wobbling. "I'm not going to act like some macho guy just because society *says I should.*"

She nodded, the smile on her face a little more wavering. I was getting through to her.

"Honesty is usually the best policy..."

A few minutes later we caved to our cravings and ordered a second bottle of wine, even though we were already through with dessert. I was feeling *alive*. Alive with anger at my ex-, at the world for being so judgemental, at myself for being so cowardly. How could I have hidden my true self away all these years. The fact that the restaurant hadn't ID'd me certainly helped too.

"I'm out, and proud, Donna. Out and proud!" I announced.

She bit her lip. "I thought you said you weren't gay. Not that there's —"

"I don't mean out like that. I'm not *gay*, I'm *bi*," I explained.

She raised her finger to her lips and looked around embarrassed.

Fuck it. I didn't care. I wasn't going to be embarrassed anymore I decided. Why should I be ashamed of what I am, of how I was created, of how I happened to be born. Screw anyone who didn't think I had a right to *be* me.

"People can hear you!" she said in a hoarse whisper.

I felt free. Freer than ever. Light headed and alive and with a feeling like I needed to do something, say something, be something. I stood up, pushing my chair back with a scrape.

"I don't care! I don't care anymore! I'm free from the shackles of society's oppression! I'm open now, Donna. I don't care who knows!" I said, then raised my voice further "I love pussy!" I declared, raising my hands. "And, I like cock! Beautiful, hard, throbbing cocks! And tits! And guys asses! And—" I breathed in sharply. "Ow!"

She had kicked me in the shins. Hard. I dropped back down to my seat, my new found energy and confidence draining from me. I began to feel weak again. My body slumped into the chair. What on earth had gotten into me?

"That's all very good, Jamie, "she said with a frown, "but this isn't exactly the place for this kind of announcement! We're not in San Fran you know."

"More's the pity." I told her.

"Drink your wine and be quiet."

I sighed. Deflated, but still with a feeling as if a burden had been lifted off my shoulders.

It was as if admitting it out loud was the same as admitting it to myself. There'd be no more sneaking around. if I dated another girl I'd tell her straight up: *Just so you know, I do enjoy a good cock in the mouth every now and then...*

Or could I even date a guy? A big, strong, man? What would that be like, I wondered.

"Umm, Jamie..."

I blinked as I left my musings and looked up. Donna was looking off to the side with a sly look on her face. So I looked to the side.

I gulped.

One of the most beautiful couples I'd ever seen in my life was standing there.

A hot, blonde girl in shorts that should have been classed as a breach of the peace and a tight top that looked like it was clinging to her with all its might. And next to her with her was a tall, moody looking guy, a real musician looking type. He looked down at me and ran a hand through his hair. I just about swooned. Was that why he did it?

Now, what did they want?

Johnny

Have you ever kept a secret so long that it became a part of you? As if your entire identity was composed of both the public part, and this other, secret part of you which no one ever knew anything about. That's how I was. Because of where I lived, the lifestyle I lived, I never could admit to that other side of me.

But now, here, in a new country, could I? Would I?

All I had planned to do was what I'd always done: shove that part of me back inside, keep it hidden, and never let it out again. This girl, Lucy, had helped. At least initially. She distracted me from my *other* desires, the ones that were kept under lock and key for fear of shame, ridicule and embarrassment. But now she had given me a chance. An opportunity.

Would there ever be another chance like this? Probably not. Opportunities like this happened very few times in a lifetime.

I was almost shaking as I held the wine glass in my hand. Could I do this? Was I brave enough, I wondered. She had been looking me in the eyes, but now her head was down. Her shoulders slumped. I think she was feeling dejected. As if she had screwed things up by telling me what she had. By admitting what she was, what she felt. She'd been brave — much braver than me. She had just come out and said it. I wonder how many people she'd told before.

I put my hand on top of hers. It was so soft. She looked up and I met her eyes.

All or nothing. Do or Die. "That's really, *really*, hot." I said.

"Wait, what?" she said one of her hands leaving mine and going to her mouth.

"I said, that's hot."

"You don't really mean that, do you?" she asked.

I felt my old confidence returning. It was like a weight had been lifted from my shoulders and I was no longer afraid.

"I do. I mean it."

She raised her eyebrows at me and bit her lower

lip. "Tell me," she said in a low voice, testing me, "tell me what you would do to me with another guy."

I gulped. Leaning in close to her so that no one could overhear us I caught a whiff of her perfume mixed with the fresh scent of her. Her low sultry voice and the fragrance together set my head swimming and I felt inhibitions floating away. I could do this.

I began to speak to her in a low voice so only we could hear. "I'd touch and kiss you everywhere, while he did the same. Four hands would caress and squeeze you, pinch you and finger you."

She looked at me eyes wide and smouldering, her cheeks flushing.

"We'd both kiss you, I would kiss your lips, while he kissed your breasts, your stomach," I said in an even lower voice, "your pussy."

"Then what?"

"Then I'd kiss him, in front of you, tasting the delicious taste of you on his lips while you watched, fingering yourself."

"I wouldn't do that..."

"No?"

"No, I'd take both of you, one in each of my hands, and squeeze you while you made out."

I felt myself growing hard under the table. It felt so *bad* to be talking like this in a restaurant. In public. But it also felt so right, and I realized I didn't give a fuck. No one could hear us with our voices low; why shouldn't we talk dirty.

"Oh that sounds good."

"Then I'd get you to climb on top of me, and force yourself into me "

I nodded, my cock straining against my jeans. "Then?"

"You'd hold yourself in me, kiss me, while he..."

She bit her lip. She was almost squirming in her seat.

"While he what?"

"While he enters you from behind."

I squeezed her hand hard, my breath fast and shallow while I listened to her impossibly hot words.

"I'd wrap my arms right around you both, dig my nails into his back, and as he pumped into you, you would be thrust into me."

I looked at her parted lips, and unable to control myself I reached over and kissed her hard. I'd never had a conversation like this. Never said things like this, or heard them said by anyone else.

Here we were, in public, in this Italian restaurant talking about me fucking her while I took another guy's hard and hot dick deep inside me.

"Then?"

"Then we fuck. I squeeze you and knead you and try and wrap my legs around you both, while he fucks us both, hard, using your cock to pleasure me."

"And..."

"And we let him fuck us, harder and harder until his young body can't take it anymore. He grabs us both tightly as he fills your ass with cum."

Shit, this girl was unreal. How could she think things like this, *say* things like this. No one ever said things like that. No one ever in the history of the world had ever said anything like that, had they? Surely not. But this girl, my Lucy, she could do it, she could say it, she could say anything.

"And as he fills your hot ass up you can't take it

any more, and nor can I. With a scream we'll all be driven over the edge and we'll collapse in a big, hot, sweaty, sticky mess.

I squeezed her hand. "Shit. We need to make this happen."

She nodded. "And there'll be more too. So much more. Both of you inside of me, you inside him, showers..."

I wondered if this moment was real. Surely I'd wake up and it'd all be a dream. A girl this hot couldn't be into all these things, these things I've never talked about with anyone before. It wasn't possible.

"Hey, what are you doing?" she asked.

"Just pinching myself. I can't believe I'm awake."

"Are we going to make this happen, then?" she asked.

I nodded at her. "Yes. We will. We have to."

I'd never felt so confident of anything in my life. I knew we had to make it happen. I knew we had to find a way to do this, and that if we did it would have a profound effect on both of our lives. We would be intertwined forever. Before I knew I liked her, liked her a *lot*, but now...

In that moment I realized that we had been destined to meet. She was the one. The perfect girl for me. Now all we had to do was find the other part.

"It'll happen if we allow it to happen," I said to her with new confidence.

"What do you mean by that?" she asked

I was speaking with authority now. With the dead certain faith of a man who simply *knows*. "If we allow ourselves to be open, to look, to see, to hear, the universe will show us."

She tilted her head at me like I was crazy. "What?"

"I'm serious, Lucy. The universe will give you what you want, if you really, truly need it and want it and just let yourself be open. I realize this now. I've been hiding all my life but now I think I finally know who I am and what I need to do."

"Uh huh. Right. The universe will provide," she shook her head at me like I was being silly. She clasped her hands together and put them under her chin, leaning forward. "I've got a better idea, maybe we can put an ad on Craigslist. You know, that we're looking for a guy."

"Maybe. But I think if we just open ourselves up to the universe..."

She interrupted me with a snort but I didn't mind. I knew, right then, that I was right. It was like the first time I truly meditated; that spiritual awakening was similar to what I was feeling now. I was seeing with new eyes, hearing with new ears, feeling with a new touch.

"You really are a hippy, you know that?"

I grinned and let it turn into a beaming smile as I looked around the room, seeing it seem to glow with energy and good vibrations. As I looked around suddenly I saw a blond head pop up over the low dividing wall.

"I like cock! Beautiful, hard, throbbing cocks. And tits!..."

Lucy tilted her head at me and gave me a look. "What the fuck?"

I couldn't quite believe it myself. I mean, I know I had just given Lucy my little talk about the universe giving you what you really want... but still, I'd expected it to take a bit longer than thirty seconds. And anyway, maybe this shouting blond boy wasn't the answer. But in my heart, I knew he was. He had to be. "I told you, all we had to do was make ourselves open and listen."

She shook her head as she rose to her feet and peered at the speaker. I did the same. We both looked at him, then we looked at each other as he sat down again, hushed by the woman he was with. She raised her eyebrows at me.

"He's..." I started to say.

"...beautiful," she finished.

I felt a lump in my throat. Like I said, I'd never been with a guy. But if I was going to pick one to be my first then *he* was almost perfect. A younger, blond surfer looking boy. No doubt an aspiring model or actor with perfect washboard abs, nice biceps and a perfect dick.

"You know, maybe you're onto something, hippy."

I nodded at her. I hardly believed it myself.

But this was it.

I knew it.

This beautiful boy was it.

Jamie

"We were wondering, " said the blonde girl.

Oh shit. What did I do?

"If you'd, y'know..." she said with slightly raised eyebrows and slightly parted lips.

I didn't know. I didn't know at all.

"Y'know?" I stammered.

"Want to... come back..." she continued.

The gorgeous guy with her was staring straight above my head at the wall, his face expressionless.

"Come back?"

"With us," she finished as he nodded in agreement, his eyes still firmly fixed above us.

I gulped and felt my cheeks get hot. Donna kicked me under the table again. This time it was a *don't miss this chance* kick, instead of *shut up* kick. They felt remarkably similar though.

I looked down at the table, feeling my cheeks blossom. Shit, what had I done. I grabbed my wine glass, tilted it back and emptied it down my throat.

What had I done. What had I done!

"Well?" she said, hands on her hips, head cocked to the side and bright blue eyes sparkling with mischief.

She was beautiful. And him! What could they want with me? It couldn't be *that* could it? But then again, what else could they want with me. They must have heard my silly little alcohol fueled speech.

"Okay?" I said meekly.

The girl beamed a million watt smile at me and the guy gave a little half-nod of satisfaction.

"You go ahead," said Donna, "I'll get this."

"Thanks."

I sat there unmoving for a moment. How was this going to work, I wondered. The girl reached out a hand. A small, soft hand. I took it. She gave it a little squeeze and in a daze I rose to my feet and let her lead me away from my friend and the safety of the known.

In front of her was him. I didn't even know his name; or hers for that matter. He was leading her with one hand and she was towing me behind her with the other.

People were staring at us as we passed through the other tables to the door, making little whispered comments and giving knowing looks to each other. I think I was shaking as I walked out, her hot, soft hand in mine. Her other hand in *his*.

What had I gotten myself into?

Lucy

Have you ever stood under a gushing, warm, shower in a dimly lit room while two gorgeous guys touched, felt, and rubbed you all over. One older and experienced who knew exactly what to do. One young guy with all the enthusiasm of youth, his hands and mouth working double time in an eager attempt to please.

It was a completely new experience for me. My body had never felt those kind of sensations. There were so, so many hands. Mine, and his, and *his*. While it only adds up to six, when you count all the fingers, the backs of the hands, the palms, the wrists, the forearms, the rubbing arms and thighs and calves it was like I was in a whole new world of touch. In the dim light my eyes were closed most of the time as if my body couldn't handle all of those different senses at once.

The guys had been a little awkward at first, but a

few puffs on a joint and some somewhat stern instructions from myself for them to strip and follow me were all it took.

Now we were together, three beautiful naked people, under one too narrow stream of water as we touched, and felt, and explored each other all over.

The soap (or rather, my expensive body wash) soon came out and we became three frothy giggling, fondling people. Our hands and body became extra slick slip'n'slides of pleasure as we rubbed and touched and occasionally licked each other — rather regretfully when we got a mouthful of suds.

And the cocks. While there were only two of them, it felt like so much more. It seemed that every time I moved my hand a giant rod of manhood ended up between my fingers as I playfully tugged and pulled at it, while another rubbed against my tummy, or lower back or ass. Both of these guys were thicker, longer, straighter, and simply more grabbable than any I could ever remember seeing — either onscreen or in person.

When those cocks weren't slipping between my fingers they were slapping against my belly, my ass, my thighs, and any other part of me they could reach. We were three horny, horny devils as we cleaned each other off, grabbing and touching feels from each other as we did so.

"This is amazing." I said.

"Oh, fuck yeah," moaned Jamie.

My eyes flickered open for a moment and I saw that Jamie's hard cock was currently between the fist of Johnny, who was pumping it up and down gently, half massaging half masterbating the younger guy.

There's something about that that really does it for me. Everyone's known that guys love watching girls get it on together forever. But you never really hear so much about girls getting off watching two guys. To be honest I didn't even know whether everyone did like it as much as me. Maybe it was just one of my weird quirks. But whether I'm weird that way or not the sight of two hot guys getting together is one sure way to get my little motor firing.

Watching the tanned young surfer have his manhood pleasured by my older, tatted up, rock star man sent a squeal coming out of my throat. I gasped as a hand slipped over my slippery breast and squeezed my slick nipple. It was too much. Too many sensations at once, with the water running over us, and so many different touches and sounds going on all at once.

"Let's get out of here," I said, gasping as a hand came from nowhere and ran between my legs, "Let's get on the bed."

There were muttered words of agreement and sounds of lips touching. I opened my eyes again and now saw that both the guys had their hot lips pressed against each other, each one grabbing the other's cock and gently rubbing it.

Shit, they weren't going to forget about me, were they? I got my answer when they broke away from each other and Johnny wrapped his arm around my waist with one hand and gently rested his hand on my upper thigh. His fingers ran backwards and he squeezed my pert pass.

"Come on." Johnny stepped out into the dimly lit room, the only light coming in through the open doorway which led to the bedroom beyond where a single solitary light bulb was burning on a bedside lamp. They had been shy at first so I'd deliberately kept the lights dim. But they were getting over it now. Oh hell yeah, they were getting over it.

As Johnny lead me out I felt Jamie pressing into me from behind, his hard cock poking into my lower back. I reached behind me and fondled his balls and cock eliciting another moan from him.

"I can't believe this is happening," said the boy behind me, "this is going to be the hottest thing that has ever happened to, like, anyone, ever," he said.

I gave his cock another reassuring squeeze. "Oh, it's real all right. And we've only just begun."

Johnny grabbed three towels from the rack and tossed one each our way while using one on his own body. He turned to face us, and we watched each other as we all tried to quickly get off at least the worst of the water.

I knew they were all as horny as me, and we wouldn't exactly be making sure we were completely dry. After a few seconds of rapid toweling I found myself sandwiched between the two guys as I was hustled into the bedroom.

I bit my lip and quivered in anticipation. There was no way this wasn't going to be the best night ever.

We all collapsed onto the bed. And froze. I realized they didn't know what to do next, they were both horny as hell but at the same time this was new for both of them. But I couldn't, wouldn't, let them feel uncomfortable again. I had to take control for a few minutes until they were really and truly at ease with all of this. While I knew Johnny could handle a woman better than anyone he clearly didn't know much about getting with a man. Even though he did seem to be incredibly turned on.

"Both of you, lie down," I commanded. They both lay on their backs.

I knelt on the bed between them, my skin seeming to glow under the dim light of the bulbs. I could see them both staring at my nude body with lustful eyes. I reached out my hands, and took hold of each of them. Both sets of eyes went wide.

"Kiss." I gave a little nod and licked my lips. I was going to get a show. "*Kiss. Kiss each other. Tongue-fuck each other's mouths." I gently, ever so gently pumped both of their dicks as I ordered them. My two boys.

They both turned their heads toward each other and their upper bodies came closer together. Young, boyish Jamie lifted his head slightly, his long, blonde hair hanging down as he lowered his lips to Johnny, who I never would have imagined being into this.

It was the hottest thing I'd ever seen. I was burning up as I watched them. The two beautiful, beautiful men began to kiss passionately as I pumped both of their dicks, squeezing them hard with lust as my body sizzled. I could hear the moaning, and breathing, as I pleasured both at the same time.

Watching them kiss was everything that pornography *isn't*. Watching it has never done it for me, but this, *this* right in front of me. The heat, the smell, the sounds the passion and the electricity in the air made me feel like I was floating above the bed as I kneeled there, naked, two men in my hands while they passionately ran hands and lips all over each other.

As I watched I saw Johnny begin to take control. To be more like the Johnny I'd known that week. One who wouldn't take any crap and was going to take whatever it was he wanted from the girl — or boy — in front of him.

He ran his hands over the younger guy's chest, and down to his cock where his hand met mine. We made eye contact for a moment and I saw that he was consumed by lust. Eyes dilated, pupils like those of an animal rather than of a man. I let his hand grab Jamie's giant, hard cock and then slipped my hand over the top of his. I could feel my man squeezing my boy as together we worked the hard dick we gripped.

I couldn't take it for too long. I was so hot and wet and *empty*. I needed to be filled, to be fucked, hard.

"I need you, Johnny. I need you in me," I whispered.

Two pairs of eyes broke away from each other and both stared at me in lust.

"*And* you," I said, meeting Jamie's eyes.

The boy Jamie licked his lips in nervous excitement. I leaned forward over them and pressed my chest down. Jamie eagerly took my right breast in his mouth, his girlish soft lips kissing and tongue swirling over my bullet-hard nipple.

I let out a squeal.

"Get behind me," I said to Johnny who wriggled out so fast he was gone in an instant.

I pulled my breast away and then met Jamie's lips with mine, tasting him and Johnny, both my men, at once. He was softer and gentler than Johnny, but oh so good. It was almost like kissing a girl. *Almost.* With his rock hard cock and surfer's chest I never for a moment imagined him as anything other than a virile young male.

I felt two strong hands grab my thighs. Johnny was behind my exposed ass and pussy.

I broke off my kiss with Jamie and using my mouth I worked my way down his body. Behind me I could sense Johnny ready to pounce, ready to force himself inside me just like I wanted.

The body underneath me was so soft and hard at the same time. An enigma. The skin like that of a baby, so gentle to the touch. But underneath was the toned, hard muscles of a swimmer. With my tongue I could sense the outline of each hard ab as I kissed my way down his sixpack to my goal.

All the while Johnny had been rubbing his hot, hard cock against my pussy lips, teasing me cruelly. But I knew he was also teasing himself. He couldn't bear to do it long, not with my hot, tight hole right in front of him just waiting, *begging*, to be filled.

I scooted down the bed a bit as I got lower on Jamie's body and finally reached my target. I hovered above him for a moment, my hot breath teasing his quivering, throbbing cock.

That was it. I think we all about reached our limit at the same time. Just as I was about to slip my mouth over him he grabbed me by my hair. I let out a gasp of double surprise.

At the same time as Jamie grabbed my hair, Johnny grabbed my hips tightly and with one stomach-curdling thrust buried his cock so deep inside me I thought it was going to come out of my mouth. At the same time Jamie thrust up with his hips and yanked my head down, forcing his massive, hard member deep between my hungry lips.

One moment I was an empty, desperate mess, the next I was filled with more cock than I knew what to do with. Jamie thrust his hips and yanked my head several times forcing me to slide up and down his hard member, before lifting me off his cock with a groan.

"Is that alright?" he asked

I let out a frustrated whimper as he held me up above his cock.

"Don't ask that again," I said, panting. Young guys were always like that in my experience. But older guys, like Johnny, knew that if I was in this state then I was begging for it and didn't need to be asked again. "Fuck me, boys," I said with a desperate moan. "Use me. I'm your fucktoy. Do me hard," I said with a moan.

I saw Jamie's eyes widen before he began to do exactly as I had commanded. Losing his reserve he grabbed me by the hair even tighter than before and forced me back down on to his cock which I greedily took into my mouth. Johnny grabbed me even tighter and fucked me harder and faster. I hoped he was enjoying the view of me getting face-fucked by his new friend.

I lost myself in it. I was their toy, their sexdoll, as they each worked one end of me. They bounced me roughly between them as they used both ends of me to pleasure themselves, and me.

The taste of the hot young cock in my mouth and the so thick and hard cock pounding into me from behind was almost enough to send me over the edge instantly. But not quite. That didn't happen until Johnny started to use his fingers to pleasure me too. As I moaned and let saliva and precum dribble down my chin Johnny used a finger to tease and work my clit while thrusting into me hard from behind.

It was too much. Like hanging off a cliff by your fingertips I tried to slow the inevitable with all my might, enjoy a few last delicious moments where I still had semblance of control, but it was in vain. Johnny's fingers working my clit, his hard cock thrusting into me from behind and the delicious taste of the gorgeous boy sliding in and out of my mouth sent me tumbling and falling off the edge to the kind of orgasm that makes you wonder whether you're going to live through it.

They didn't care. I was no longer in control of my

body, and I was merely being held up by the strong hands grabbing my hair and hips as they fucked me, literally, senseless. I let out a mewling kind of screaming groan as my body convulsed.

They thrust themselves into me harder and harder, prolonging my delicious torture and leaving me paralysed, my only control being the frantic panting breathing I was doing to keep myself conscious as they fucked me to oblivion.

Finally. Finally in a series of violent thrusts they both began to climax. Johnny and Jamie came together into my own still quaking body, filling me up at both ends with their hot delicious seed and causing my body to fall off that cliff again. I swallowed greedily at the sweetness that Jamie was forcing into my mouth, but was unable to keep up and some dripped down my chin and onto the damp white sheets below.

I'd never felt like *that*. I think it was the fact there were two of them, both into it, into me, into *each other* that did it. Having that much pent up desire in one room was unbelievably arousing.

"Holy. Shit." I said as they finally allowed me to

collapse onto the bed.

They lay down beside me, one on either side.

"Come here," said Johnny, pressing his lips against mine. Our tongues met and I gave him what I knew he wanted — a taste of Jamie. After a moment, he lay back, head on the pillow.

I turned to the other side. Jamie was grinning at me. Then he pressed his lips against mine too.

We all three lay on the bed, panting, exhausted, satiated for now. But I knew there would be more. A lot more. We'd barely even begun to satisfy all the different cravings we each had.

But the most important one had been fulfilled. We'd found each other.

Johnny

I woke up the next morning when Lucy gave a little squeal. Memories of the night before flashed through my brain. I tentatively opened my eyes and saw her sitting up on the bed, cross legged, completely naked, and holding her smartphone in both of her hands.

She sensed that I was awake and turned toward me without any shyness, "This is amazing."

"What is?" I asked

"I just got an email from my professor. There's a way. There's a way I might be able to still graduate early."

"Oh yeah? So, you'd be done this summer?"

She bopped her head up and down enthusiastically, her blonde hair fluttering around her beautiful cheeks. Behind her the blonde boy, Jamie, still seemed to be completely out of it.

"Yeah. It seems all I have to do is find an

internship. If I can do that, then I'll be able to get enough credits to graduate early, and so I won't have to come back next semester, and I won't have to take on a student loan."

"Or work as a stripper?" I asked.

She smacked me on the arm. "Shut up. I told you I wasn't going to do that."

I grinned at her and raised an arm, gently running a hand over her breast.

She licked her lips and looked at me. Then gave a little frown. "I really should deal with this. He's given me a couple of options, and I've got to start sending some emails and making some phone calls. Shit, and I've got to get my resume in order. Man, I got so much to do."

"Come on, surely you've got time for a little bit of morning loving?"

She shook her head. "Sorry. I know that if both of you wake up I'll never get out of here. Anyway, you don't need me."

"I took her hand in mine and lowered it to my hard cock.

"Oh yes I do."

She squeezed me gently, and then let go and sprung to her feet. I looked up at her, standing above me in all her naked glory. Her smooth, tanned, nude body was like that of a goddess above me. I wanted nothing more than for her to sit down again. Preferably this time straight onto my cock. Or, just as good, my face.

"Come on, sit down," I told her.

She jumped off the bed. "Nope." She started toward the bathroom door. "You want some ass? You've got some right there." She nodded her head towards the sleeping Jamie. "He's gorgeous, and you just know he would love to be woken up with a dick in his ass."

I looked over at the sleeping boy. The sheets were pulled down and I could see the curve of his back reaching to glorious buttocks. I wondered what it would be like to slip my dick in there. I'd never done that, never done anything like that. Despite all we'd done with Lucy last night neither of us had penetrated the other. Yet.

"But you have to promise me something, all right?" Said Lucy.

"What's that?" I asked.

"You have to tell me everything," she said raising her eyebrows with the final word.

"You'd like to hear that, huh?" I said.

She nodded and blew me a kiss. A moment later she was through the bathroom door and I could hear the hot water immediately begin flowing in the shower. I sighed because she had gone and there'd be no morning pussy for me. But then my eyes flicked down again to the sleeping boy. She did have a point.

I edged closer to him, my hard cock tight in my hand.

I scooted down the bed a little toward the two glorious orbs of his ass. Tentatively I moved my mouth forward. I began to kiss him, and a moment later I was tonguing his ass. I heard him moan, and gently shift his position so that my tongue could delve deep into him. He was half awake above me. Now that he was wet with my saliva I moved up my body and push my cock between his lips. He knew exactly what I wanted and quickly coated it with saliva, sucking me and slobbering on me with two rosy lips.

With my dick now sopping wet, and his ass the same, it was time for me to do what I'd only ever dreamed of. Fuck a hot young guy in the ass.

Jamie moved on to all fours, with his head down on the bed. He displayed his gorgeous athletic ass toward me, and began working his own cock with one hand.

"Do it. Fuck me in the ass," he said down toward the pillow, "You'll be my first."

"Your first, huh?"

He let out a sigh as I ran my hands over that firm pair of buttocks.

"You know what?"

"What?"

"I've never done this either." It felt odd to be saying that. To actually being honest again. It seemed that the night before a new chapter in my life had begun, a time when I could finally be honest.

"Hurry up. I need it. Put your big, hard, dick in my ass and fuck me."

I didn't need telling twice. The boy underneath me was furiously pumping his own cock as I pressed the head of mine up against his tight little hole.

"Fuck. Me."

I squeezed him tightly by the hips, as I began to push the head of my cock against his tight little hole. It wouldn't go. I pushed harder and he let out a squeal. I grabbed my dick with one of my hands and started to push it. Finally it started to go in. But not fast enough, apparently. With a thrust backwards Jamie pushed his arse towards me, and my dick entered heaven.

I let out a gasp of my own as the head of my dick completely penetrated his tight little hole. He was so hot, and so tight.

I leaned forward and pushed the rest of the way inside him.

Grabbing his shoulders now I held him tight and began to fuck him. Seeing the naked, younger man below me moaning as I pushed my long hard hot cock into his tight little ass hole was an incredible turn on. Most guys don't know what they're missing out on. I swear if you've never fucked a beautiful little teenage surfer boy in the ass, you haven't lived. Don't get me wrong, girls are great – Lucy is outstanding. But this was a whole other level, a completely different experience. It's like cake and ice cream — they're both fantastic. And together, like last night...

I grunted with pleasure as I thrust into him. Underneath he was moaning too. I could tell that this young guy was loving every minute of it. He loved having my long hard cock thrust into his tiny little hole.

"Oh my God. That feels so good," he said. He let out another moan as I thrust into him again.

"You like that? You like it when I fuck you in the ass?" I asked him, my voice raspy and breathless.

Our bodies were sweaty again now. I dug my fingers into his hard shoulders, feeling his so soft skin, almost as soft as Lucy's, as I pressed my fingers into the damp flesh.

I knew I couldn't take much of this. It wouldn't be long. Sometimes people have the idea that you should always savor your first, make it last as long as possible. Fuck that, I thought. I wanted to come all up in this boy's ass as fast as possible. I wanted to fuck him hard and fast and explode inside him. There would be other days, other chances where we could take our time. But today, this time, I wanted to get thirty-something years of secret out of me and into him.

As I looked down I saw him biting the pillow. That was it. He was also furiously squeezing and rubbing himself, letting out little squeals. I couldn't take anymore. With the final few hard thrusts I let out a guttural moan of my own as I felt myself explode up in his tight little hole. It seemed I set off a chain reaction in him. A moment later I saw his release spurting out underneath. As I filled up his ass with come, he covered the sheet underneath. God knows how much fluid Lucy, me and Jamie had spilled in this room since last night.

I collapsed on top of him, my chest resting on his back, our skins wet and slick.

"Oh. My. God."

"Fuck yeah." I answered.

I don't think I'd ever come as hard as that. Years of pent-up sexual frustration had just been released in a couple of minutes of violent, sweaty, ass sex with this beautiful blonde boy.

Just as I was getting my breath back there was a hammering at the door.

"Come on, open up, I know you're in there."

Chad.

Johnny

I looked around, panicked. Lucy burst out laughing. She'd been standing by the bathroom door, watching me fuck Johnny in the ass.

"That was quite a show," she said. "Jamie, why don't you hop in the shower?"

He let out a moan of agreement and headed across the room. My eyes were on his beautiful, curved naked ass the whole way until the door closed behind. Damn, I needed some of that again soon.

"I'll find you later, okay?" said Lucy.

I nodded and we kissed on the lips. Everything was going so *right*, I thought. As she got to the door I wrapped the bedsheet around my waist. She opened it and Chad burst in, walking right past her as if he didn't even see her. Lucy gave a shrug, rolled her eyes and gave me a grin as she headed off.

"Okay, I got some good news and some bad news," said Chad as he entered the room.

"Hit me with it."

"The bad news is, we found your bassist. We found Si," said Chad.

"Thank fuck for that," I told him, "that monkey you gave me last time was absolutely useless. So why's that bad?"

Chad nodded understandingly. "The thing is, he said he's done with it all. He's quit. He's quit the band, he's quit the music, he's quit everything."

"You're shitting me," I said.

"Nope," said Chad.

I smashed my palm against my head. Why was all this happening now. I had enough on my plate without having to worry about this shit. How could he be abandoning the band at this time?

"it doesn't make any sense."

"Welcome to Hollywood, baby."

I let out a sigh. "We're not even in Hollywood, Chad" I told him. "Okay then, so what's the good news?"

"Ah well that's the thing, isn't it? Actually I think I'll save it for later. Let's just say, you're not going to be disappointed with the new bassist you're getting."

"When we did the last auditions you told me had a whole bunch of talented people lined up. They all sucked. Now you're just going to hire someone one without me even auditioning them first?."

"Yep. And you're going to thank me for it."

I gently nudged him toward the door and he obligingly stepped backward, halfway out into the hallway.

Before I could get him all the way out he stopped me.

"Meeting room A, in fifteen minutes, everyone's going to be there. Make sure you are too. Big stuff going down, buddy."

I let out a sigh and managed to close the door on him. But as one door closed, another one opened and a freshly showered toned and tanned surfer boy with just a white towel and a cheeky grin on his face exited. He looked good enough to eat.

"Shit," I said running my eyes over him. "don't you go anywhere. I've gotta go deal with some shit, but when I get back…"

He tilted his head at me. "It's my turn next time."

I raised my eyebrows at him. Did he mean what I thought he meant? What would it be like, I wondered, to lie under him while he put his long, hard cock up inside me. I'd had girls tongue me, and finger me there to my great delight, but what would it be like to actually take a full sized cock. I shivered in anticipation.

I gave him a half nod and headed towards the bathroom. Just before I got there he pulled the sheet from around my waist, and I let him. He stood to face me, being a couple of inches shorter than me he was looking up at me with two gorgeous, sparkling blue eyes. He placed two hands on my ass and gave me a squeeze. Then he turned and push me towards the bathroom.

I didn't want to go, but I didn't have long before I was supposed to be downstairs and I had to get showered first.

"Later," he said to me.

I nodded with a sigh and went to wash off, anticipating our next meeting and hoping Lucy would be able to join it.

Johnny

Standing on the stage, listening to the crowd roar as I strummed the final few cords, my plectrum and fingers moving in a perfect fluid flow, no thought required. I breathed in the hot, energy filled air enjoying the final few moments of the show. The small but eager crowd screamed with hoarse voices and bounced with tired limbs as the final few notes faded away. It was done.

And today's bassist had barely fucked up at all. This wasn't the one Chad had promised me, his 'secret' bassist was still a few days away. But this guy today had been okay.

Just as the lights started dimming to signal the end of the show, I saw Jamie and Lucy near the front. They were standing together, closely. I realized I didn't mind. I wasn't jealous of the younger guy. I was just pleased to see them both there. Both watching me.

"Great show, man," said Jamie with a grin.

"Thanks," I said as I wrapped my arm around Lucy's shoulder.

Jamie tagged along behind us as we headed out.

"Some of the boys are going into town for a drink. Want to go?" I asked

"No thanks. Can we just go back? Can we get our own car?" asked Lucy. She sounded tired. And miserable.

I didn't mind. I'd spent enough of my life going out drinking with those guys. Going back to the hotel after the show actually didn't sound like a bad idea at all.

"Let's just have a pizza in the room. I'm too stressed to go anywhere today."

While we waited for the taxi Lucy told us her news."So you remember this morning, I was excited, because my professor had sent me that email?"

"Yeah, what happened?"

"Basically he was just being a big cock-tease."

"How's that?"

"His email told me that if I could arrange an internship for the summer I could still get my credits and graduate early, debt-free."

"Sounds perfect. What happened?"

"Well, it turns out, that every last business our school has a relationship with is already full for the summer except for one."

"Yeah? What was the matter with that one?" I asked.

"It was a paid internship."

"Yeah? That sounds about perfect, doesn't it?"

"Yeah, you'd think, but..." her voice trailed off, teasing us with suspense.

"What? Is it interning in a strip club?"

She giggled. "Worse than that."

"Worse than that? I've got to hear this..."

"When they say it's a paid internship, what they mean is *I* have to pay *them*."

"What the hell? You pay them? That's not an internship, that's like — I dunno — slavery or indentured servitude or something."

"Yeah. Fuck that. So I told them they could shove it."

"So, no hope then?"

She shook her head dejectedly. Just then the car pulled up. It was a large black SUV.

Jamie turned to us as he reached toward the door handle and said, "Wait till you hear about my day."

"Yeah, what did you get up to?" asked Lucy as she climbed into the back.

I followed her into the car, stepping up and sliding onto the soft leather seats. These cars were pretty swanky.

"I got a shoot coming up. A real modeling gig, finally. A beach shot. I'm going to be modeling a new range of surf swimwear," he said, the excitement palpable. From what I'd heard he'd moved to LA with plans of becoming a model or actor, but none of that had quite panned out yet.

"That's great," I said.

"That's hot," said Lucy and she turned to him, "see if you can snag me some bikinis."

"Hey, I'll *buy* you a bikini," I told her.

She let out a laugh. "You just want me to model it for you."

I gave a grin and a nod. "Yep. And maybe show

you off if we ever get to a beach."

She hit my arm and giggled. At the same time I felt a hand on my thigh. I looked down, and it was Jamie, his perfect young hand resting on my upper thigh. I half shook my head in disbelief — I wasn't sure I'd ever get used to this new, exciting phase in my life.

Seeing my headshake Jamie went to lift his hand away but I placed mine on top, stopping him. It was nice having the hand there.

"I've got some news too," I told them. "Get this...".

"What?" asks Jamie giving my thigh a squeeze, his voice a little higher than before.

"So, Chad was talking to me today about his plans. You know this tour was supposed to just be these little shows like today, right?"

"Uhhuh."

"Yeah."

"Well, get this: It was all just a tease. These little shows were to build up some word of mouth, some coverage, they were all just foreplay.

"Foreplay, huh?" said Lucy, perking up.

"Yeah. We're adding another date. Only this time it's going to be big. Like *really* big. A giant, outdoor, free show. Come one come all. Tens of thousands of people."

"Tens of thousands? Holy shit," said Lucy.

"That does sound pretty rad. A free show though? No pay?" asked Jamie.

I shrugged. "Yeah, I guess. But that's not the point. If this actually goes off, it won't matter. With a crowd that massive our presence is going to be huge, and then we'll explode on the charts..."

"Your presence? That sounds like Chad-speak," said Lucy with a grin.

I couldn't help but laugh. She was right. That was Chad-speak.

"Yeah, well. He's right though I think. Oh, and there's more..."

Lucy looked up at me. "More?" she asked with a twinkle in her ridiculously blue eyes that now seemed gray in the dimly lit interior of the car.

"Yeah. He's got someone big to play bass for this

show. Really big."

"Like who?" asked Jamie with genuine curiosity.

"He wouldn't say exactly—"

"Asshole."

"Dick."

"Yeah, I know," I continued, "but I think it's... Flea."

"No shit?" asked Jamie sounding genuinely impressed.

"Who?" asked Lucy sounding genuinely unimpressed.

I sighed and turned to Jamie, "We've got to get this girl an education."

She smacked me on the arm. "Hey. I'm a straight 'A' student who was going to graduate a year early. I've *got* an education."

Straight A's huh? I hadn't realized that. Most impressive. "A *real* education, a <u>musical</u> education."

She sniffed. "I got the new Beyonce."

"W—" I managed to stifle a screaming diatribe before it had barely begun and I heard Jamie let out a laugh.

Luckily that's when we arrived back at the hotel; Lucy's education would have to begin another time. As we pulled up, just like the night before I felt butterflies in my stomach again. Was I really going to take this young guy back to our room again? It didn't seem possible. Years of suppression made me immediately think it couldn't happen, it couldn't be real, but then I glanced to my right — the beautiful young guy next to me tilted his head and let his fingers drift up to my crotch, giving it a squeeze. It was like a shot of something amazing straight to a vein — it was real.

* * *

"I'll order the pizza, you go take a shower," said Lucy.

I nodded and headed to the bathroom door.

"And hurry up, or we'll start without you."

I turned back to face them. "The pizza, or..."

Lucy raised her eyebrows at me. "Or," she said with a finality that made it neither choice nor option.

Blood rushed through me as a million possibilities flashed through my head in rapid succession and I realized something. I didn't mind if they did 'start' without me. The idea of these two beautiful young blondes getting it on, fucking, didn't bother me at all. If I came back from my shower and saw them both naked and...

"Go ahead. I want to see something interesting when I come back."

Just before I closed the door I saw them turn to look at each other and two sets of arms reach out.

Horny bastards.

A few moments later I'd stripped off and was under the steaming hot water, running my hands through my hair and letting the stress of the show wash away. There are only two things better than a hot shower after a show to help recover from the massive outflow of energy you've just been put through. They are meditating and a good, long fuck.

That reminded me, for the first time in years I hadn't actually meditated for two days straight. I could feel my mind becoming more and more cluttered with all the new shit that was happening to me. I needed to get some quality *me* time soon.

I briefly considered using that moment. But...

A moan loud enough to pierce the bathroom door *and* the sound of the rushing water reached me. I let my hand run down idly to my cock and felt it rapidly surging. As I began to wonder what the two beautiful blondes were doing out there a thought crossed my mind.

"That's it!" I banged my fist against the tiles in triumph. I had an idea. A good one. One that could solve Lucy's problem *and* relieve that nagging thought that had been hiding at the back of my brain for the last few days, only occasionally being allowed to the front to really bother me: What's going to happen next week — is this *really* just a week long fling?

No, goddammit, it wasn't.

I emerged from the bathroom a few minutes later, skin still damp, heart pounding, to see one of the sexiest sights I'd ever had the pleasure to see in person. Scratch that *the sexiest sight I'd ever seen in person.* Thoughts of my brilliant idea fled from my mind like they'd been blasted out by a shotgun and my dick immediately began to get hard.

"Hey—" said Lucy, her words disappearing into a

gasp.

Jamie

The bathroom door closed on the guy-of-my-dreams while the *girl*-of-my-dreams gave me a look like you wouldn't believe. What an amazing, weird couple of days. I had to keep pinching myself to make sure I was awake, and then pinch myself again to make sure I hadn't just dreamed I'd pinched myself.

"You're very cute you know," said Lucy, running her fingers through my hair. The smell of her so close to me was intoxicating.

"Not handsome?" I asked with a semi-pout.

She shook her head and ran her hand over my cheek, fingers running across my lips.

"One day you will be. Maybe when you're thirty, or forty. But right now you're cute," she paused, looking into my eyes, "gorgeously cute."

I'll take it.

"You're not cute," I lied. She was just inches away from me and when she raised her eyebrows threateningly I felt like I was in danger for my life. "You're sexy as fuck," I finished with a smirk on my face.

My cheeks blossomed with relief when she gave me a smile. I reached out and put a hand around her waist. How far could I go with her, would I dare to go with her, with her *boyfriend* in the shower right beside us? I didn't want to ruin *this*. The best thing that has ever happened to me.

She was dressed as she often seemed to be in a tight, midriff-baring t-shirt and little shorts. Her legs were impossibly long and slim for her frame and those few inches of flat, tanned stomach made me think of every hot girl I'd ever seen on the beach and then blew them all away in my mind.

"You shouldn't swear, you know," she said, tapping her index finger on my lips. "You're too sweet for that."

"Really? But you swear all the time," I retorted.

"That's as maybe, but I want you to remain our cute boy. Okay? Your mouth is made for much better things."

Her telling me what to do sent a little thrill through me. And what better things did she have in mind?

"Now, for swearing in front of a lady," she stifled a giggle, "kneel."

Her voice was stern and didn't brook no messing. I did I as I was told and let myself fall to my knees. I looked up at her and saw that her eyes were full of mischief. I wanted to reach out and touch her but I waited to be told what to do next instead.

"She put her hand on her hips. "Undo my shorts."

I tentatively raised my hands to the waistband of her tiny shorts, and with shaking fingers undid the top button.

She tapped her foot.

With my hands still shaking I continued and undid the last two buttons. I looked up at her.

"Well?" She asked.

Before I could pull them down there was a knocking at the door. "Pizza!"

She sighed and walked away. I started to get up, but sensing my movement she turned back toward me,

"Stay," she said.

She opened the door and I caught a peek of the delivery boy. I saw him glance down at Lucy's tiny shorts, open to reveal the sexy underwear underneath. His eye caught mine and he grinned. I blushed. She paid him and put the pizza on the table. There was something else she wanted first.

"Now, where were we?" she said when she was standing over me again.

I didn't need to be pushed any further. I put my hand to the waistband and pulled down her little shorts. Underneath was revealed a lacey white thong. I felt my tongue run across my lips in an involuntary movement of anticipation.

"I've had a really long, stressful day. And now I need my stress relieved."

I nodded up at her and then brushed the blonde hair out of my eyes after it fell, blocking my view.

"Well, go on then." She said, biting her lower lip.

She really wanted me to do this. She wanted me on my knees, in front of her glorious body, giving her head to relieve her 'stress'. I could hardly believe it.

I didn't need to be asked again. Not with my face inches from the beautiful, barely covered pussy of one of the sexiest girls I'd ever met. My hands went back up to the waist of her sexy underwear but before I pulled it down I couldn't resist kissing her through the soft fabric. The smell of her invaded my nostrils and it was divine. As my lips pressed against the thin fabric it was so flimsy that I could feel the outline of her pussy lips underneath. She let out a soft sensuous sigh.

That sharp out breath from her was all I needed. Unable to resist the delicious yet sexy aroma emanating from her hot pussy I feverishly put my hands back around her waist and yanked down her thin panties. My nails scraped the sides of her thighs as I pulled them down, causing another sharp intake of breath from her.

She stepped out of both the shorts and panties, but remained in her high heels as she stood over me, looking down, her bare pussy just a few inches away from me. I admired her gorgeousness for a second too long; she put two hands into my hair grabbed my head and yanked me into her tightly.

If anyone ever asks me what heaven tastes like,

I'll tell them it's like this: having your desperate tongue between the legs of a gorgeous twenty-something college coed as she eagerly pulls your mouth into her hot, wet pussy — while her *other* boyfriend showers next door. I couldn't get enough of it and she let a squeal escape from her lips as I eagerly ran my tongue up and down her hot, wet slit. My hands ran up her calves, over the backs of her knees, over her upper thighs and to her deliciously round ass.

As I gave her ass a squeeze, and buried my tongue deep inside her, I felt her knees buckle a little, and then hold. I was now leaning back, my abs flexing with the strain, as she began to grind herself into my mouth. I couldn't help but pull her in tighter, my fingers squeezing the roundness of her buttocks. My tongue buried deep into her, and then withdrew, and she let out a gasp as she ground herself into me, most of her weight pressing onto my face.

Her legs buckled and even my strong abs weren't enough to hold her up forever. I quickly grabbed her around the waist to slow her descent as I fell back onto the floor, lowering her slick lips back onto mine. She put her hands down on the floor on either side of my head and began to grind herself against my tongue.

My hands roamed her body, feeling her up under her tight T-shirt, running over her smooth back and squeezing her firm ass. All the while she ground herself against my lips and tongue as I desperately tried to read her signals and give her pleasure.

I heard her panting fast a few times and adjusted the rhythm of my tongue to try and match her. This led to a squeal of what sounded like frustration coming from her.

She pushed herself down on to my tongue again and I felt like she was trying to suffocate me. What a way to go it would be anyway. There couldn't be a better way, could there?

Just as I seriously began to worry whether I would ever breathe again I heard the bathroom door open.

Lying on my back I could just about see the upside down image of our glorious, gorgeous rock star as he re-entered the room. He was standing there naked, hands on his hips as he surveyed our antics with a twinkle in his eyes.

"Thank god you're here," said Lucy.

Cool air rushed across my face as she rose to her feet. I lay underneath, panting as I regained my breath. I saw upside-down Johnny give her an inquisitive look.

I sat up, licking my lips wondering what was going to happen now. Was he going to kick my ass?

Lucy kicked off her high heels and stepped toward the bed, pulling her t-shirt off over her head as she went.

"Come on," she said to Johnny as she jumped gloriously naked onto the bed.

I saw him glance at her then me.

"You too," she said to me and I grinned. Panic averted.

Lucy climbed onto the bed, her head resting on the pillow, her naked legs pulled up to her ass.

"Over here, quick," she said to Johnny.

The rocker walked toward the bed and I admired his nude form as he moved toward the girl we both adored. My tongue ran over my lips involuntarily yet again as I saw his long, hard cock poking out ahead of him. Although I could still taste her on my lips, I desperately wanted to taste him too.

As he climbed onto the bed I saw Lucy open her legs invitingly and Johnny immediately knew what to do. He put his head between her legs and she immediately let out a squeal and dug her hands into his hair.

"Get your clothes off..." she gasped out in my direction.

I rose to my feet and quickly did as I was told, pulling off my t-shirt and jeans revealing what I know is a pretty sexy body — if you like slender, toned surfer guys that is.

"...and suck his cock," she commanded.

How had she known that was exactly what I'd wanted to do?

When I was fully naked I joined them on the bed, crawling under Johnny's legs while his mouth was kept busy above. I lay flat on my back, the rocker's lower torso and rock hard cock above me. He was so busy eating Lucy out I wasn't sure he'd even noticed I was there.

I soon made him notice. Taking his, long, hard cock in both hands I pulled it to my lips. As I reached out my tongue to tease him he shifted his hips and pushed deep into my mouth. It felt like his cock was sliding to its rightful home as he slid deep into me.

Lying underneath him I couldn't maneuver well, but that was okay. Johnny knew exactly what he wanted to do and began to slide in and out of my mouth, amazingly managing to keep his mouth focused on Lucy while he also kept his cock focused on sliding in and out of my eager, hungry and willing mouth.

The flavor and scent of the hot English rocker merged with that of Lucy making a heady cocktail in my mouth. It tasted better than booze, better than drugs, better than se— wait, this *was* sex.

I wrapped my arms around the waist of my current lover, squeezing his hard ass and encouraging him to fuck my mouth however he wanted. I wanted him to use me for his pleasure, I wanted to satisfy him. I wanted to be his boy-slut.

I heard Lucy let out a gasp and then Johnny raised his head — sending his cock deep into my mouth

— and said something though I couldn't hear what; I was too busy taking so much of him into my mouth.

"Jamie..." I heard her say breathlessly.

With my mouth full of rockstar cock I couldn't say anything except let out a sound of acknowledgement.

"Fuck him..." she let out another squeal.

"... in the ass..."

I gulped and became aware of my own rock hard cock pressed up against my lower abs. Johnny reached down and gave it a squeeze that sent a shiver through my body. He lifted his hips and slid out of my mouth which immediately felt sadly empty.

I guessed that was his seal of approval.

Gorgeous girl pussy, a nice hard dick in the mouth, *and* a hot man's ass to fuck? Did life get any better than this?

Johnny

Apparently the boy wasn't as good at eating pussy as me. Not that that surprised me, I had heard I was, I quote, *the fucking best* several times in my life. As I tasted Lucy yet again, this time I got a flavor of my young friend too.

From the squeals and moans and clamping of the soft thighs around my head I knew I was doing something right. Of course.

When the boy climbed underneath me and opened those soft cherry lips of his, well, it felt like my cock was coming home as I slid it right into that soft, hot and eager opening. Is there anything better than a cocksucking surfer boy taking it in the mouth while you eat out a gorgeous college student? I don't know if there is, but I had an idea for something I'd never tried.

I lifted my head up from Lucy for a second, forcing my cock deep into the boy's mouth as I changed position.

"Get him to fuck me," I said to her in a hoarse whisper.

She looked at me with rosy cheeks and a wicked glimmer in her eye."Really? Hell yeah."

She was excited and turned on by the idea, but I was still too... reserved? Unsure of myself? To actually say it myself.

"Jamie..." she said, as I rewarded her with a flick of her clit with my tongue causing her to let out a gasp, "fuck him..." I did it again and she squealed, "in the ass."

Good girl, I thought. I had an immediate pang of regret though when the boy slid out from underneath me and my cock left his sensuous mouth.

I don't know much about this stuff, having hidden this side away all these years. I think I read somewhere (accidently, I swear) that a lot of people are *tops* or *bottoms* but I hadn't really got it. I mean, to me, both things seem incredibly sexy. Sticking your dick in the tight ass of a gorgeous-bodied young stud? There's not much sexier. But then, on the other side, lying down, and getting them to do it to you... man... the idea of being so vulnerable and getting the *other* person so turned on that they'd *want* to do that is such a turn on too.

And of course, over the years I've been lucky enough to have girls tongue me while they wanked me off, or to slip a finger inside while we fucked or they blew me. Loved it every time.

Two warm hands grabbed me by the hips, the thumbs pressing into the flesh of my buttocks.

"Do it," said Lucy, "put your boy cock right in his rockstar ass and fuck him."

Shit, I thought, she shouldn't have been able to get out a whole sentence like that without squealing or gasping. I put my head back down again and this time was rewarded by her thighs clamping my head like a vice.

I've always been good at multitasking. Maybe it's from years on the stage, playing the guitar while also singing and at the same time leading the band. Now I had to put that multitasking skill to the real test.

"Fu—" I breathed sending hot breath over Lucy's most sensitive areas. The boy had placed his mouth on me and begun kissing and tonguing me. Being tongued in the ass by what I knew to be a beautiful tanned and ripped surfer was one of the wildest things I'd ever felt.

And I immediately wanted more. I spread my thighs a little more and Lucy read my cue immediately.

"That's enough... he's... ready," gasped out Lucy.

Was she a mind reader? She was reading me so well it was hard to comprehend that she was just another living and breathing person — at times like that it was more like she was just another part of me, like we were two aspects of the same being.

It turned out Jamie didn't want to hesitate either. After a final generous tonguing that left me sopping wet I felt something pressing against me. Pressing hard. I knew what I wanted right then more than anything in the world — his thick, so-hard cock buried in my ass.

Resting my head on the bed and using both arms I reached behind me and wrapped them around his awesomely curved buttocks and pulled him toward me. I was going to have his cock in my ass, and I was going to have it there *now*.

"Oh *fuck*," said Jamie.

I let out a deep groan of pleasure of my own.

His hard, thick cock penetrated me, filling me up like no finger or tongue could ever do.

"Oh, yes..." breathed out Lucy.

My eyes met Lucy's and I could tell she was almost as turned on as me. *Almost.* She had that crazy dilated-pupils look that girls get when they're super-turned on and a rapturous look on her face.

"This... is what... I always wanted... to watch..." gasped out Lucy in between the long slow licks I was giving her.

Behind me I felt the boy push harder and just when I thought it was impossible to fill any more full, I did, as he squeezed his hands tight around my waist and buried himself all the way inside me. Something happened when he did and I felt... something... I'd never felt before. He reached a place of pleasure that I didn't know existed forcing a gasp of air out between my lips which made Lucy squeal too.

I needed more of that. And fast.

"Fuck me, fuck me hard," I said from between Lucy's delicious legs.

I guess he heard me this time because the boy began thrusting in and out of me, so, so, deep into me.

Jamie began to pant as he fucked me in the ass, I began to breathe deeply too and Lucy was still a breathless squealing mess as I worked on her tight and wet little pussy.

"Harder," said Lucy, "Fuck him harder... and faster..."

I squeezed Lucy's thighs tight with my hands as my body began to be wracked with ever stronger waves of pain and pleasure as the surfer behind me had his way with me.

Lucy said something I couldn't quite understand and a flicker of movement caught my eye. I looked to the left and, bizarrely, a good looking girl I'd seen around our shows was there. I watched her grab a bag of weed from the bedside table and scurry away, clearly embarrassed by what she'd been seeing.

Huh. That was weird.

But that wasn't something I could, or wanted to, dwell on. I was busy getting fucked in the ass by a smooth and hard bodied stud. I bit my lip as he thrust particularly deep inside me and with a start I realized I wasn't as good at multitasking as I'd thought. I'd been neglecting Lucy.

Luckily she was the kind of girl willing to take things into her own hands, literally, and she had started to finger herself. Her delicate fingers were now fully engaged in fucking herself.

She noticed me noticing her. "You got distracted," she said, now able to control her speaking better.

All I could do was shudder and gasp as the boy drove into me hard. Her eyes lit up. She was really enjoying the show.

"Now," she said, "I want you to put it in me."

"I'm... busy..." I managed to strangle out.

She raised her eyebrows and bit her lip and somehow I managed to understand. She wanted me inside her... while Jamie was still fucking me. Crazy.

She began to scoot down the bed and I lifted my body up with my elbows, inadvertently meeting one of Jamie's thrusts and sending him slamming deeper than ever inside me.

A moment later I had the gorgeous naked body of my young fuck-buddy-turned-girlfriend beneath me. I don't think my cock had ever been harder in my life, at least not while I had so little self control.

She got her arms between our two bodies and slipped two hands around my cock. With some manipulation I felt the head run across her slick folds and then a moment later I entered nirvana. Jamie pushed into me with just the right force and direction to bury my own cock deep into Lucy.

I was the middle part of the most gorgeous and sensual sandwich ever created. My lips met Lucy's and I realized it wasn't possible to ever have a moment more intimate than this. I was filled up from behind while also filling up the girl underneath me with my own harder-than-it-had-ever-been cock.

Jamie's hard fucking of my eager ass had slowed and we became a sensual threesome. I didn't know how it worked, but his body and mine worked together in harmony to thrust in and out of her and me.

We were a wild, sweaty bunch. So much skin contact. So much sweat and saliva and precum and juices. It was impossible to know how long we were like that, an entangled intertwined set of three lovers giving and receiving more pleasure than seems probable, or even possible.

We were slow at first, Lucy and I kissing so deeply I sometimes wondered whether we'd ever escape from each other's mouths. Finally I felt like I couldn't take any more, like my body would just dissolve and I'd disappear forever if I didn't get any release soon. I broke off the kiss for a fraction of a second.

"Faster," I commanded.

"Yes, sir," said Jamie.

Sir. I liked that.

Lucy tried to wrap her legs around us, just about managing to hook her ankles on the curve of my other lover's ass.

We thrust and pulled and pushed and kissed together in unison, a perfect fucking trio. I pushed myself harder and harder into Lucy, each time I got as deep as I could go Jamie pounded into my ass from behind sending another final push deep inside her. Each time it happened she squealed or moaned or gurgled or yelped or gasped; a tiny little sex-noise making machine under me as we slammed into her.

Jamie panted hard behind me and I knew he couldn't take much more of my ass, he needed to come. Me too. I yanked on Lucy's hair and held her tighter than ever as I fucked her hard.

From the strangled yelps and sounds she was making you'd have thought we were killing the girl underneath us, and if it wasn't for her still eager tongue and pulling ankles I'd have been worried for her.

With a last gasp I yanked Lucy's hair hard and buried myself inside her. As I felt myself begin to spurt hard into her tight pussy Jamie gave a yell and a final thrust that felt like he was trying to get into Lucy's pussy through me.

My vision blurred and suddenly I wasn't just orgasming in my cock and balls, but deep inside me too.

"Fu—" I couldn't even make a word. My whole body seemed to contract and explode as I was rocked by a series of sensations I'd never even imagined. Lights exploded behind my eyes as I felt my surfer boy cum in my ass and I found myself making guttural, animal sounds like I'd never done before.

What the hell had just happened, I wondered.

Whatever it was, I knew I wanted more of it. A lot more.

Us three together were magic. Three puzzle pieces that fit together perfectly. I knew I couldn't let this thing end, let it fail.

It was meant to be. *We* were meant to be.

Lucy

We were sitting in the dining room of the hotel. A place that had seen James Dean, Marilyn Monroe, John Wayne and a host of others in its glory days more than sixty years previously. Now it was a tired-looking room that served a rather average breakfast buffet: rubbery bacon and eggs, soggy toast, cheap jam, strangely watery milk, disappointing coffee and fruit that would have been fabulous had it been served two days earlier.

We were the only members of our whole group here. It seemed the rest of the band didn't quite make it to breakfast, and I hadn't seen Jase or Lonnie or any of the other biker slash security guards in here either. Jase had mentioned it being *too classy* for them. It wasn't.

"Mother*fucker!*" said Johnny as he joined us. He'd just been waylaid by Chad.

"Uhoh?"

He slammed his fist down on the table, his hair shaking as he did so. His face was tinged with red.

"What's wrong?" asked Jamie.

"Chad."

"What'd he do now?"

He shook his head with exasperation. I knew they had put a lot of faith in the big-talking but infuriating little man. I hoped he hadn't completely screwed them over.

"He told me he had *Flea* from the Red Hot motherfuckin' Chili Peppers to play with us. He doesn't. It was all bullshit. He was starting a rumor to build up interest for the big show."

"No shit?" I asked.

"That's low."

A deep sigh of disappointment as he slumped over the table. Then he sat up straight again, putting on a brave face. "Still, I get to play with Lonnie again."

I gave him a curious look. "*Lonnie?* From the Sons?"

He nodded. "He used to be in the band, once, a long time ago, back when we were young. He quit it all and moved out here though."

"You think he can play your songs?"

Johnny shrugged. "He was always a natural, picked up songs like—" He snapped his fingers.

"You're taking a big risk, aren't you?"

Johnny shrugged. "I figure it's fifty fifty."

"How's that?"

He gave a wry smile. "Either he, and we, kick complete ass and put on the show of our lives and become mega-stars. Or..."

"Or..."

"Or we crash and burn in spectacular fashion. That would probably make Chad happy too — we'd be all over the websites and blogs and whatever you call them. But either way, we succeed or we fail. So it's fifty fifty."

Nice logic, I thought and laughed.

"You can do it, I know you'll do great," said Jamie with an award-winning smile.

"Thanks. But who knows. We'll see. Hey, if we crash and burn, maybe I'll come be a stripper with you," he said nodding his head toward me.

I kicked him under the table. "I told you, I'm *not* going to be a stripper."

What he'd said sent a pang of remorse through me. The band's flight out was only a few days away, and then what would happen? Would that be it, for us, would it all be over?

It would. There wasn't any other way. We all knew it and we'd all studiously avoided talking about it. I was going back to my miserable over-priced college for a final semester, Jamie was going to be here doing his modeling or acting or whatever and Johnny — beautiful, rockstar Johnny, was going back to his home country and then who knows where.

Placing a chewy forkful of egg in my mouth I knew I couldn't stop myself. I was going to do it. I was going to talk about it.

"After the show, after... a few days," I began.

Johnny sighed while Jamie shifted awkwardly in his seat.

"I thought we weren't going to talk about that?"

"I know, it's just — I don't know. I can't help it. It feels like what's happening now is *it*, the high point of my life. When you leave, and then I leave, this dream will be over. And that's all this is, right? A dream. A silly American fantasy for you and a summertime fling in LA for me."

He shook his head, reached over and took my hand. "No, it's not just a dream. It's real. This is real. I'm real, *he's* real," he said nodding his head toward Jamie, "and all that's happened is real."

A feeling of morose negativity was running through me and I felt tears beginning to well. This wasn't like me. Not at all. "But if it was real it wouldn't end. Not like this. Not before we even had a chance, a real chance."

"Lucy, please. Let's not give up hope yet. A few days ago you hadn't even met me, *us*, who knows what will happen a few days from now?

"But we *know* what's going to happen. You're going to get on your plane, and I'm going to drive back to college."

He shrugged and gave me a mysterious smile. How could he be so blasé about this? Maybe he didn't care about me, about *us* the way I thought he did.

"You don't care, do you?" I said, before angrily forking some more bacon into my mouth.

He leaned over and took my free hand. "I care. Trust me, I care. A lot. More than... more than I ever have, for anyone. Really."

"Then stop acting like you don't."

"Just because I have confidence in fate, in destiny, doesn't mean I don't care. Please, let's just try and enjoy these last few days and see what happens."

I didn't answer. He didn't seem to understand at all. Maybe it was a man thing. Or maybe it was a Johnny thing. I didn't know. And what about Jamie? We'd only just met him but after the few nights we'd had together I was sure he was feeling the same connection that I was. That he was the third ring of the triangle.

He gave my hand a squeeze. "Trust me, okay?"

I shrugged dejectedly. Sure, I'd trust him. But I also trusted in facts, and they were that this time next week me, and him, and our new boytoy were all going to be apart. That's just the way it was.

I slowly chewed the eggs and bacon and wondered if it was possible that he was right. What if there was a way? Could I simply do what he asked, close my eyes and give in to blind faith in destiny, I wondered.

Well, crap. Today was his big day. The day his band played on a stage in front of tens of thousands of people. Maybe I could do it, for him. I was too young to stop hoping, to stop dreaming. Fuck it. Maybe he was right.

"Okay. I trust you. It'll all be okay, won't it?"

He nodded.

"It will."

And I realized I believed him. I really believed him.

Lucy

This was it. The big show. The air was warm and thick with a feeling of anticipation. In front of the rapidly setup stage the crowds had gathered and there were more people than I could ever have imagined in one place. I'd never been to a music festival, or a big outdoor show like this, so it was my first experience of seeing this many people all come together to see a band. And not just any band... the band of which I was dating the lead singer.

Nicole and I had been guided by her boyfriend, the biker president and guy in charge of security, to a section off by the side of the stage. He didn't want us out in the crowd. Too unpredictable he said — and we all knew that was code for *dangerous*. If it had been some random guy, instead of my best friend's boyfriend, I would have made a snarky comment about it being his job to make sure it *wasn't* dangerous, since he was in charge of that... but I knew he was a standup guy and doing the best he could do in the limited time that Chad had let them have to get it sorted.

"Better than the last few shows, huh?" said Nicole.

I nodded in agreement and took a sip from my plastic cup of beer. "Damn right. I don't know why they did all those stupid little shows in those skanky clubs and bars."

She nodded. "Right. Chad said it was to build anticipation, make them unique and underground or some crap."

"Yeah, well. This is more like it. How many people do you think are here?"

She shrugged. "Loads. You know I saw this on the news this morning? They did a whole story on the band. I guess I missed some of what they'd been up to. Did you know Lonnie broke the jaw of some state senator's son? And their missing bassist was in some crazy underground MMA fight... other stuff too. I mean, I guess it's 99% Chad getting them in the media any way he could. I swear he was encouraging them to do every stupid damn thing they thought up just to get on some crappy blog or for a local news affiliate to cover them."

I took another gulp of beer before replying. No matter how skeevy Chad was he *had* still managed to get this mega-crowd together for Johnny's band. And I was grateful for that. I guessed that was partly why Johnny was so confident things would work themselves out between us all. I swallowed another sip of the deliciously free and said, "He may be a slimy little bastard but I guess he got the job done."

"I suppose. Where's your boyfriend?"

"Backstage somewhere I guess?"

"Not that one," she said, poking me in the arm. "The cute one."

I giggled. "He couldn't make it. He's got a modeling shoot today. It's pretty wild, huh? Both of them together."

"Yeah. So are you like... serious with both of them now, or what?"

Why'd she have to bring that up.

"We're just having fun," I lied. While I'd told Johnny I trusted him to make everything okay, I didn't really feel like having that conversation with Nicole right now. She was *way* too practical to just accept that we'd somehow workout how to stay together in the next few days. She'd want to know all the practical details, which simply didn't exist. So I'd just play it cool with her for now.

She nodded, "That's good, right? I was worried you were really falling for Johnny. But they'll both be hundreds of miles away soon, right?"

There was a crack and suddenly my hand was wet. I'd squeezed the flimsy cup and it had snapped under the pressure. "Maybe," I muttered.

"Shit, let's go get a new one. How long have we got?"

"Who knows. Maybe Chad will make them delay for hours to build more anticipation or something."

Nicole frowned at the thought. "He better not. My thighs are killing me already."

We started heading off to the 'secret' keg stash for the staff.

"What's wrong with your thighs?" I asked.

Nicole's face bloomed and she rapidly stepped

ahead of me. "Nothing," she said over her shoulder.

I giggled. *Nothing*. Yeah right. More like crazy sex sessions with the biker club president. I recognized that blush anywhere. Maybe I'd tease it out of her later. *My* thighs were fine today, maybe she could give me some tips.

Johnny

Finally.

Finally.

FINALLY!

"FINALLY!" I yelled into the microphone.

They didn't know what I was talking about but they went wild anyway. We were standing on the stage under the early evening California sun and in front of my band were thousands, no, tens of thousands of people. Tens of thousands of people there to see us, to see me.

We've been a band for nearly fifteen years (though going through a few name changes along the way), and we've played small clubs, we've played pubs, we've played bars, we've played a couple of weird punk weddings, we've released a few minor successes, and we even played at the Reading and Leeds festival a few times, allbeit on the minor stages at the less popular times. But now, finally, we had a real audience. Not just a few dozen or a couple of hundred, but thousands upon thousands, upon thousands.

And they were screaming. They weren't just here, they were eager, they were hungry and they wanted to rock.

I looked behind me at my band and I knew it, I just knew it. All of them, including Lonnie, our bassist-turned-biker-turned-bassist who hadn't played with us in a decade, were ready and raring to go. My eyes met each of theirs and we were all connected: our minds, our brains, our hearts. This show was going to go off. We exchanged nods, but it was the connection I made with my eyes that did it — that gave me the confidence to know that this show was going to be the best damn performance we'd ever given, that we ever could give.

I waved my hand horizontally in the air and a silence dropped over the crowd. I felt my stomach drop in awe. What a feeling of power, to be able to do that to a crowd with just a wave of a hand.

"Good evening," I said in my most English voice (they loved it), "do you want to hear a few tunes?"

Lifting my microphone stand and twisting it in the air I pointed the microphone toward them. It was just a gesture to get them to respond. And holy shit did they respond. It was like a roll of thunder or a herd of horses galloping across the plains. When the noise of their screams hit it was like a wave of sound and I swear I stumbled as the vibrations poured over me, under me, around me, *through* me. Now *that* was energy. It filled me up. I stretched up and out, absorbing it all, letting their passion fill me up until I was fit to burst.

Then I stood back down, held the mic in it's stand and with a subtle hand signal let my lead guitarist Neal know that it was time to begin. And he did it perfectly. He strummed a single string on the guitar and let it resonate across the sea of people. Then my drummer, Rabbie, smacked his drum with a single stick.

The crowd were standing on tiptoes, aching for us to begin.

I counted in my head and knew the guys behind me were doing the same. *Three... two... one...*

I bounced into the air and seemed to hang like

Jordan as the band exploded into a glorious cacophony of guitars and drums behind me. Time seemed to slow as I stared out into the ocean of bodies ahead of me, seemingly held in the air by the force of the music coming from behind me. There was no drug high like this, *nothing,* like this.

Then time returned to its normal state, I dropped back down to the stage with a thump and opened my mouth in a rock scream.

I had more energy and power than I'd ever had in my life. I flew across the stage, bouncing, and jumping, pouring my heart and soul into the mic. Behind me the band gave their all into their instruments — and then somehow managed to give it even more.

Perfect. Perfect, perfect, perfect. Me. Us, the crowd, the setting. I lost myself in it all and became one with the music and the crowd and I wasn't the only one. I knew what we were doing was going to be a life-changing event for so, so many people in the crowd. This wasn't just a show, this was a once in a lifetime spiritual-bloody-experience.

Jamie

"Alright, you're doing great. You're gorgeous. If I could bottle that smile I could quit this and retire."

It was Jean-Luc Trudeau, *the* photographer for shoots like this - attractive young guys and girls in swimwear, underwear, beach shots — whatever. And he'd just called *me* gorgeous. *Me!* It wasn't like there wasn't competition here. I was surrounded by a gaggle of beautiful fifteen to twenty-five year olds and it was *me* he was speaking to.

"Didn't shoot you before, yes?" he asked.

"Actually, you did," I told him, "about three months ago? The CK thing?"

He gave a little frown of concentration, before shaking his head.

"Now you have a — how you say in English — je ne sais pas."

I just about exploded. Everything was going so *right* for once. My thoughts flashed back to the previous few nights and what we'd done, and then back to the present, to the shoot.

"There you go again. That look. That *twinkle*. Ah, to be young again," he said, shaking his head. "Now, go put your arm around her waist," he gestured to a beautiful dark haired teen.

I did as I was told and for once I barely noticed how beautiful my co-model was. *Barely*, I wasn't completely dumbstruck.

"Let your finger go lower."

I spread my finger*s* just below the string that wrapped around the skimpy bikini bottom waist.

"Yes, now it looks like you're going to pull it off. You want to fuck her, you're *going* to fuck her, yes? Let the camera see that. *Tell it* to my camera."

As the camera began to snap away I glanced at the girl and she gave a shy but inviting smile. It reminded me of Lucy — not because she gave shy smiles like that, but because she did quite the reverse. Lucy was the very opposite of reserved, and the other night, when she'd stood above me, and told me what to do to her, *commanded me... ordered me* to pull down her shorts, her underwear, ground herself into my...

"Perfect! You are a natural!"

The girl turned to the photographer and smiled at him, pleased with the recognition. I saw her open her mouth to thank him. But —

"No. Not you. You are mediocre. Acceptable. Him. *He* is a natural."

I felt her slump against me. Poor girl. I felt too pumped up on my own recognition though to really care too much.

"Okay, now you," he said while gesturing to a tall African-American guy called Jake, "and you," he said gesturing to another guy with a similar build to me but with dark hair, "and my muse," he said looking at me with a wistful look in his eye. "Next we are going to do the towels."

We came over and huddled around the genius photographer while the rest of the models wandered off to drink some water or smoke or whatever else they got up to on their breaks.

"The designer and I have a vision for this shot. It will be so, so, beautiful!"

We all nodded thoughtfully. To be honest though, I doubt any of us actually cared about the *vision* or the *concept* or whatever other buzzword was being dropped. We cared about the exposure, the additions to our portfolio, our reputation and of course our paycheck. But in order to get all those things we had to *pretend* to care about the vision and the concept. So pretend we did.

While I'd been daydreaming about what we really wanted, as models slash actors, I realized that I'd actually missed most of what he was saying, though I still had the appropriate, thoughtful look on my face.

"... so want to do something fun, but risque. Sexy but still legal for a billboard. Some shots will also be for the magazines, yes?"

We all nodded. Whatever. We just needed directions.

"So, this one is a little, how you say, 'omoerotic. Then we will do some with the ladies. These first ones will be in some select markets, in San Francisco, in Paris and so on."

We could all see the excitement in his eyes. It

was no secret that the photographer liked his young men, and perhaps that was why he was so good at capturing us on film. It didn't matter though. He could look at us all he wanted as long we got what *we* needed out of it too.

"Homoerotic huh?" said Jake, whispering to me, "What's he going to do? Make us suck each other's cocks?"

Jean-Luc's eyes whipped over to us and I smashed Jake on the thigh with my fist. I didn't need him messing up the famous photographer's new found love for me. He gave us a frown and a wagged a finger at us in a kind of endearing disapproval.

"Now, what you will do, is simple," he picked up one of the large surf-branded towels and held it in front of his body. "You will hold the towel, like this," he said holding it in two hands in front of his waist. "And then, you will drop it, like this, yes?" He demonstrated the simple concept by letting the towel fall to the floor.

"Just drop the towel?" asked the dark-haired guy.

"Yes. And, as you do so you 'ave to 'ave a cheeky grin while you look at the other guys."

"What *kind* of cheeky?" I asked.

"You know. Cheeky. Like, you will suck my cock, cheeky."

Cheeky indeed.

"Then, my camera will catch that moment, that magic moment when the viewer realizes that you have nothing underneath — *nothing*..." he leaned in toward us, "but, they can't quite see anything delicious. Yes?"

"So it's a nude shoot?" asked Jake, "My agent says we get paid extra for that."

"It's *not* a nude shoot, because in the photos we will see nothing," said Jean-Luc.

"But we *will* be nude, right?"

"You will have the towel!"

"But we're *dropping* the towel, so we'll be nude, so we should be paid extra."

Jean-Luc frowned. He may be a good photographer but he was also renowned for being tight with the cash. He gave Jake a disappointed look and said, "You disappoint me. You could be a slight talent but your attitude brings you down. Middling. That is all you will ever be, *middling*. Now, shoo." He waved his hand to send Jake back to the rest of the relaxing models. "*Linda*," he yelled to his assistant, "get me the Indian one!"

While we waited for Raj to join us Jean-Luc gave me a smile and walked toward me. What did he want now, I wondered.

"After this I need you to come to my office," he said, nodding his head toward a small RV that he apparently worked out of.

"Oh, yes?" I asked wondering what he wanted but not wanting to be too blunt.

"Yes. I have something to ask you. Something," he leaned in and whispered in my ear, "*special* to ask you about."

Uhhoh. I wondered what *that* could mean.

Lucy

I smacked Nicole's arm again. She turned to look at me. We both just shook our heads. Again.

What more could you do? We were both blown away. The band was absolutely, crazily, on fire. We'd jumped, we'd hugged, we'd screamed — shit — I'd even *cried*. I couldn't believe this was the same band. We'd enjoyed the previous shows we'd seen but this, *this* was on another level.

I looked back at the stage and shook my head again. Johnny was shirtless now and I knew tens of thousands of adoring fangirls were aching at the thought of him. But he was mine. *Mine.* I'd put my trust in him and now I knew I'd given him my heart as well.

"This next one..." he said from up on the stage before stopping to sip some water, "is for the most beautiful girl in the world." He turned to look at us. "Lucy."

My knees buckled but Nicole saw and grabbed

me by the arm. She raised her eyebrows at me and gave me that *Oh my God* look and I think she squealed, but who knows with how noisy it was there.

There were a mixture of roars of approval and boos from the crowd. I guess there were a few people jealous of me. A few *thousand* people jealous of me. I felt a warm rush spreading from the pit of my stomach and filling my entire body. Like the afterglow of an orgasm. There aren't many men who can do *that* with just words, right?

The other girl, Karen I think her name was, who was standing with us gave my arm a supporting squeeze. She was the girl who'd come in while I'd been, ahem, having fun, a few nights previously with Johnny and Jamie. I think we'd shocked her but she seemed to be over it now. It turns out *she* had been seeing Lonnie. It was like everyone we knew was hooking up lately.

Nicole tapped me on the arm and indicated she wanted to speak about something. *Great idea, let's have a chat next to the stage at the world's biggest rock concert.*

She cupped her hands around my ear and yelled

something completely incoherent. It wasn't just loud where we were, it was an absolute cacophony of guitars, drums and Johnny singing. Any kind of verbal communication was out.

She pulled out her phone and began typing, and after a few seconds held it up for me to read.

Atmosphere scary?

I gave her a quizzical look and she waved her hand toward the back of the crowd. What did she mean? The atmosphere of the show had been *amazing*, completely electrifying today. How could she say it was bad? All I could see was people having a great time, jumping around and waving their hands to my boyfriend's band.

Listen.

I snorted. She lowered her head, raised her eyebrows and gave me a stern look.

I listened. Oh. Oh shit.

While the noise coming from the speaker banks may have made it too loud for us to talk, she was right. It wasn't that there was a new noise, it was that one of the noises we'd been hearing had shifted somewhat: the noise of the crowd.

Coming from the back it was no longer just the screams of excited fans. There seemed to be one section that was more screams of anger, or fear. It's a subtle difference, one that's hard to notice in a crowd, but I guess Nicole was more tuned into these things than me. She always *was* the sensible one.

There was a lull on the stage as one song ended. I saw Johnny cup a hand to his ear. He had some kind of earpiece so that Chad could talk to them during the show. He'd told me he was going to *'ignore everything that little twat-face tells us'*, but from the look on his face it seemed like he might actually be listening to him.

He held up three fingers, then two, then one, then....

The crowd roared and whatever disturbance Nicole had identified before was drowned out by the fans at the front. They had launched into *On Your Knees*, their most famous song. Then came another tap on my arm.

Nicole indicated the edge of the stage where her

boyfriend was making an urgent hand signal. He held his index finger straight up in the air and made a circle. From our time hanging out with his MC, the Sons of Mayhem, I knew what that meant — it was time to go.

They played this song *fast*. In the other shows we'd seen they really dragged it out, they let the guitarist have a long solo, they repeated the chorus a few extra times, they teased the crowd at the beginning with false starts. Not this time. Wham, bam, thank you ma'am and the song was over.

The crowd had changed. Like a switch had been flipped. There were now two kinds of people there: those who wanted to fight and make a scene and those who were rapidly becoming terrified by the flying bottles, angry shouts and violent pushing and shoving. And the second group were making just as much trouble as the first in their frantic efforts to escape.

Peering at the stage I saw Lonnie barreling toward us. Johnny waved his hand at me and I didn't need prompting twice. I clambered up the side of the stage and headed over to him.

"Great show," I said half serious and half

ironically.

He grinned. "Real rock 'n' roll, right?"

He wrapped an arm around my waist and started to lead me off the back of the stage. But I had to take a moment to look out. I doubted I'd ever get the opportunity to stand on a stage in front of so many people ever again. Even if they weren't there for me. There was the most amazing view of the crowd and they were like a swarm of angry ants whose nest has just been stomped on. The edges of the crowd were melting away as hundreds of people fled in every direction. But the middle was a huddle of angry soldier ants letting fly with fists and kicks and flying bottles.

"Come on, let's go," said Johnny. He was squeezing my arm so tightly it hurt.

I could only just about hear him. Even though the sound of the music had faded, he was still almost drowned out by something else — I looked up at the source of the noise. Overhead a helicopter was roaring low over our heads. I stared up at it as it flew behind the stage and landed on the flat empty ground back there.

"In *that*?" I asked.

He nodded. "Another happy surprise from Chad."

That guy. Looking back at where I'd been standing I saw Lonnie had hopped down and was now leading Nicole and the other girl hurriedly away.

A stray bottle flew at my face and I ducked, just about moving away in time. Assholes. At the front of the stage a bunch of the bikers were stopping anyone from climbing up, though it was clear they'd have to regroup and fall back soon. There were simply too many people for just a handful of even the toughest bikers to handle.

"Come on," he pulled me again, and I this time I let him. I may be a bit of an adrenaline junkie but I'd had enough excitement for now.

We climbed over electrical cables and around stacks of music-related boxes and equipment. Between two piles of leftover scaffolding there was a clear path to the helicopter which had now settled on the ground with its side door open for us. We made our way carefully toward our exit.

"Step off, bitch," said a gravelly voice, from the shadows of a pile of unused equipment, "*he's mine.*"

What the fuck? A grizzled looking middle-aged woman wielding a short scaffolding pole had stepped out in front of me.

"What the hell?" I asked in confusion.

"He's not yours, *Lucy*," she said with venom. "He's mine."

The crazy lady swung the metal pipe menacingly. I couldn't tell if she was on some kind of drugs or just fucked in the head but I knew I didn't want to get too close. She had a thin white mustache and a ragged scar on one cheek. Her hair looked like she'd cut it herself — in front of a broken mirror. And her eyes were dripping hate.

I looked at Johnny. He looked at me and shrugged his shoulders. "She's right. I'm her's."

"*What!?*" I blurted out. He'd fuckin' lost it!

He stepped toward the hag with a smile. Her mouth dropped open like she didn't quite believe it. He opened his arms to hug her, and she did the same, dropping the piece of scaffolding pole as she did so. Ah, I thought, I get it.

Johnny went in for the hug with one arm, and

when her view was blocked he waved his other hand frantically behind his back toward the helicopter.

I didn't need telling twice. I wasn't going to try and fight some bitch twice as big, twice as old and almost as mean as me.

As I ran past the woman came to her senses and realized her twisted version of reality wasn't actually true. "Hey! Where you going, *whore*?"

Looking over my shoulder I saw Johnny spin her around and release her, sending her stumbling backward, a look of apoplexy on her face. One tottering step, another, then she finally lost her balance and fell onto her ample behind.

"Stupid bitch!" I yelled over my shoulder. I'm pretty witty when I'm mad, huh?

At the door of the helicopter I waited for Johnny to catch up.

"For a minute there I thought you were going to trade me in."

He grabbed my face with two hands and held it an inch from his. "Never."Then he pressed his lips against mine and we kissed under the whipping wind of the helicopter blades.

"Get *in!*" yelled some spoilsport.

He held the kiss another few seconds longer. It wasn't enough — it never is.

We clambered inside, strapped ourselves in and a few moments later I went for the first helicopter ride of my life. As we soared into the air I felt a tear run down my cheek. Johnny saw and wiped it away with a thumb.

"Don't worry, we're safe now."

"Are we, I asked?"

He nodded. "I'll always keep you safe."

Johnny

I lay back on the soft white bed in our suite at the Beverly HIlls Four Seasons. Chad had told me we deserved an upgrade for our last few days and I hadn't been inclined to disagree.

I was on the left side of the bed, warm and freshly scrubbed clean and naked. My cock was being delightfully fondled by the multi-talented Lucy who was doing the same to gorgeous young Jamie who lay on the other side of her.

This was the life. And now, to put the cherry on top.

"Lucy, Jamie," I said.

Lucy gave my cock a firm squeeze by way of acknowledgement Jamie gave a sexy *mmhmm*.

"I told you before I believe in destiny, I believe in fate, I believe that people who are meant to be together *will* be together..."

"Shit," muttered Lucy and her hand left my cock.

I reached over and grabbed it and put it right back on there. I wasn't having that. She clasped me angrily and I held my hand tight over hers. I was giving her *good* news.

"You're both coming with me."

"Oh?" said Jamie, apparently not overly enthused.

Lucy was even worse.

"I told you, I'm going to graduate. I'll be the first one from my family to ever graduate from college and I'm *not* going to drop out now."

Feisty little minx.

"You don't have to. Please, listen to me." I gave her hand (and myself) a squeeze. We both turned our heads to face each other. Her eyes twinkled with hope tempered with suspicion that I was going to ask her to drop out.

"How?" she asked, her voice dubious but her face excited.

"I spoke to my fairy Godmother..."

"Who's *that*?" asked Jamie.

"Chad, I answered."

They both giggled.

"And Lucy, I got him to make some calls. I got you an internship."

"What? How? Where? You know my college is pretty picky about what they'll accept..."

I grinned at her. This was the best bit. "You're going to be working as an intern, helping to manage a certain *internationally famous* rock band."

She raised her eyebrows and I saw the corners of her mouth twitching. She was desperately trying *not* to break out into a massive grin. She didn't quite believe yet.

"Chad has arranged it all. And he's cleared it with your college. *And* we've already applied for your work visa. Lucy, you're coming to London."

She lifted her hand up into the air, made a fist and smashed it into my chest.

"Holy fucking shit! I love you!" She pounced on me and pressed her lips against mine like she was trying to push them inside my head. Hot, sexy, and delicious as always I had to stop myself from shoving my cock inside her right then and there. I wasn't quite finished yet. I wrapped an arm around her and squeezed her ass.

"And Jamie," I reached over with my free hand and squeezed his arm. He rolled over toward us and propped himself up on his side, with one hand closed into a fist supporting his cheek.

"Yes?"

I couldn't help it. His lips were so rosy and red I pulled him toward me and kissed him. It was different to Lucy, but so, so sensual. Man, I wanted my cock inside *him* too. Or the other way around...

"What?" asked Lucy.

Oops, I guess I got distracted. It was hard *not* to with these two gorgeous bodies around me.

"You're coming too," I said to Jamie.

His lips curled up in an almost knowing smile. Cocky little...

"I am, am I?"

I nodded. "Yeah. You're going to be a roadie."

There was a snort from Lucy and Jamie immediately began shaking his head. Obviously Jamie didn't *look* like your typical roadie, but so what. He may not be the most muscular of dudes but if he put some effort in he'd be able to get it done, and he'd grow with the job.

"I'm *not* going to be a roadie," he said.

This wasn't going how I'd planned. They were *both* supposed to be grateful for the strings I'd pulled to keep us together. We may not have known each other for long but I knew without a doubt that we were supposed to be, *had* to be, together. And I'd been doing my damndest behind the scenes to make sure that happened.

"Jamie, please—"

"I'm not going to be a roadie because..." He let his words slide away, teasing us.

There was a slap of palm against skin. Lucy had slapped him on his naked thigh.

"Because what?"

"Because I've been invited to London with Jean-Luc."

"*What?*" asked Lucy in disbelief, "Really? The photographer? What the hell! That's amazing!"

"I know, right? What were the chances of that happening?"

They both had stupidly happy grins on their faces.

I didn't. Mine was more of a knowing, satisfied smile.

"What's that look for?" asked Lucy.

"I told you."

"Told me what?"

My hand roamed over her breast, brushing her hard nipple. "I told you. Destiny. Fate. Nothing can keep us apart if we're supposed to be together."

She laughed. "That's still bullshit. But I'll take this lucky coincidence."

"Come here," I said to both of them.

I pulled them both in toward me, and we lay there together, arms gently wrapped around each other, three exhausted but elated bodies on soft, crisp white sheets.

It's a confusing world that we live in, with so many people telling us what's right, what's wrong, what's moral, what's not, what the best way to live is and what mistakes we need to avoid. But we all need to find our own path.

I didn't know where our path was going to take us, but I know where our individual paths had been, that we had been brought together by destiny, and now our paths were intertwined and interlocked and going forward we would be together. Even if Lucy technically only had an internship for now, and Jamie technically only had a few modeling jobs, it wouldn't matter — the universe would make sure there were ways for us to stay the same path.

We held each other tight.

Life is crazy, but if you've got the right people along with you it's a hell of a ride.

Epilogue

Dear Nicole,

How's it going? Things pretty much suck here. I've basically been living out of a crappy five star hotel having champagne breakfasts every day while having ridiculous amounts of sex with my two boyfriends; when I'm not working to help manage the hottest band in the world. It's real lame.

I hope life isn't too dull without me over there. I can't wait to come back and visit. It looks like my internship's going to be pretty long so we'll be able to graduate together after all.

Let me know all your news ASAP! I bet life's much more exciting there than in boring old London.

Love and kisses

~Lucy

Yo! End of Book Bit

Hey,

Nikki Pink here.

UPDATE: The stuff below is now out of date, but feel free to read ahead anyway! The book I mention below is out now and called AWOL. See the "Also by Nikki Pink" at the end of the book!

Now back to the out-of-date End of Book Bit!!:

Thanks for reading this far!

Anyway, my next book is coming super soon. Really. I know I've said stuff like that before, but this time I mean it. I've had some like... issues... but I've got over them, mostly. So now I'm back to work. Work, work, work! The book I'm working on at the moment is best one yet, I think.

It's got action, it's got a good story, it's got a super sexy biker and an innocent young girl. It's a kind of older(ish) man / younger woman romantic suspense. And, I'm already mostly done on it!! Yep, the old Nikki Pink who actually… you know… wrote… and released books… is back in town with a vengeance.

And I ain't slowing down. I've got tons of things planned for the end of this year and into the beginning of the next. Tons.

So to all of you who have supported me over the years, thank you! I'm sorry I've been a bit of a disappointment… but that all changes now! Yee-haw.

So strap yourselves in. Let's do this.

To make sure you get my next book for just .99c or free join my mailing list at http://www.nikkipinkwriter.com/mailing-list.

And keep reading the following few pages to find out how to get on my ARC list and about my other books =)

See ya,

Love and kisses (if that's what you like)
~Nikki

The Rocker, the Boy and Me

About the Author

Nikki Pink is a college professor and writer, now living in East Asia. She has previously called Pennsylvania, USA, London, UK and Western Australia home, but doesn't know where life will take her next...

You can find her on Facebook at http://www.facebook.com/NikkiPinkWriter/ or at her website, www.nikkipinkwriter.com.

Also by Nikki Pink

Standalone Biker Romance:

AWOL - A Badboy MC Biker Romance

The Sons of Mayhem series:

Sons of Mayhem 1: The First Novel

Sons of Mayhem 2: Chaser

Sons of Mayhem 3: The Full Force

Sons of Mayhem 4: Never Give Up (This is the next 'Jase and Nicole' book)

The Rocker, the Boy and Me (Sons of Mayhem Spinoff) (AKA *"The Lucy Book"*)

Sons of Mayhem Books 1-3 Boxset

Made in the USA
Coppell, TX
26 January 2020

14988471R00185